SANTA'S REJECTS

ZOE CANNON

TABLE OF CONTENTS

INTRODUCTIONS

We're all familiar with heartwarming Christmas tales. The ones where the spirit of Christmas softens everyone's hearts, and the good and the deserving get their due. We love these characters! We cheer when they get their Christmas miracles, as well we should. It makes us feel good inside.

But hang on. If the spirit of Christmas is about love and charity and helping those who need it, doesn't that apply to everyone? What about the people who are harder to like? What about the ones who aren't particularly good or deserving? Are they the exception? Tidings of comfort and joy for everyone except you over there—is that how it goes?

That hardly seems like the Christmas spirit, does it?

The stories in this collection are about the people who don't normally show up in the heartwarming stories. In one story, the devil shows up for Christmas dinner, and the matriarch of the family has to decide how far her "everyone is welcome on Christmas" policy goes. In another, an angelic prison guard sneaks a demonic prisoner out on Christmas Eve so they can both enjoy the holiday for once. And in another, an elf stages a coup against Santa so the naughty children can get something on Christmas morning besides a lump of coal.

These stories are more than a little irreverent, but they also have more than a little heart. Snark or no, I believe in those heartwarming Christmas stories. I believe in love, and family, and the power of an act of kindness—for everyone.

Even—especially—the ones who are hard to love.

A Hell of a Christmas

Marcy's younger daughter had said she would be bringing a guest to Christmas. At least she had warned them of that much. Marcy only wished she had told them her guest was the actual devil.

The devil sat at the dining room table, sandwiched between Jess and Marcy's older daughter Carly. Marcy tried not to stare as he held out a hand and asked—in a voice more polite than she heard from any of her own family members on most Christmases—if someone could please pass the mashed potatoes. If not for the bright red skin and the horns protruding from the top of his head, not to mention the tail that hung down off the side of his chair to brush along the floor she had spent all yesterday afternoon scrubbing, she might have approved of her daughter's choice of dinner guest. He was certainly more polite than that boy Jess had brought last year, the one with so many piercings in his ears it was a wonder he had any skin left in them.

The devil caught her staring and gave her a wink. She flushed and looked back down at her plate. "I suppose we've all got the same question," she said with a nervous laugh. "I may as well be the one to ask it." She cleared her throat. "Are you... that is, you bear a striking resemblance to..."

Jess scowled at her. "Have you got a problem with how he looks?" she demanded. "You never give my friends a chance. I remember those looks you kept giving Logan across the table last year. Just because *you* don't like piercings—"

"it wasn't the piercings," Carly interrupted with a sigh. "It was the fact that every third word out of his mouth was an expletive. Not to mention how he kept going on about his *brilliant* career plan to lay out traps for vermin and then sell them door to door as exotic pets."

"They weren't vermin, they were *raccoons*—"

"If you chose better friends, maybe we wouldn't have a problem with who you brought to dinner," said Carly. "For that matter, if you chose better friends, maybe you would be doing a bit better for yourself by now." She lowered her eyes to look at her younger sister over her glasses. "You do realize everyone is the average of the five people they spend the most time with."

Just made a rude noise—one that most certainly did *not* belong at the dinner table, especially not at Christmas. "Well, not everyone wants to be an overachieving corporate drone," she said, and stuck her tongue out for good measure, as if she were still five years old.

Marcy's mother gave a sniff from the other side of the table. "In my day, girls had standards," she said. "Girls from good families like yours didn't even consider dating boys who were obvious bad sorts." She narrowed her eyes at Jess's dinner guest. "Let alone embarrass themselves by bringing those bad sorts to a family dinner."

Just rolled her eyes. "In your day, 'bad sorts' just meant someone who wasn't lily-white. And I guess not that much has changed, has it?" She patted the bright red hand of her dinner guest. "Anyway, we're not dating. He just needed a place to go."

Marcy's mother screwed up her face like she had swallowed a worm. "In my day, girls also didn't talk back." She poked at the mashed potatoes on her plate. "And they knew how to make proper mashed potatoes," she added, with a side-eyed glance at Marcy. "These are full of lumps. And too salty, to boot."

"That didn't stop you from getting seconds," Marcy couldn't resist pointing out. Jess snorted.

"Oh, please," said Carly, looking at Jess. "You bring a guy to Christmas dinner, and you expect us to believe there's nothing going on between you? Besides, he looks like just your type." Her sharp voice turned the words into an insult.

Jess scowled. "We are *not* dating. I've sworn off men for at least the next six months. I saw him on campus moping around while everyone else was packing up to go home. We got to talking. It turned out he had nowhere to go."

That did sound like Jess, Marcy had to admit. She had always been one for bringing home the wounded baby birds.

"The devil is in college?" she couldn't resist asking in a faint voice.

"I believe in bettering oneself," he said with a nod in her direction. "You're never too old to keep learning."

"That reminds me of how I met my first wife," Marcy's father said to Jess, resting both elbows on the table to lean in closer. "I was about to leave campus to spend the holidays with my good friend Marilyn Monroe. It was purely platonic between us, of course, but she did know how to throw a party." He waggled his eyebrows. "But then I saw Jeannie, looking like it was the worst day of her life. And no wonder. Christmas Eve, and she didn't have a soul to be with."

Marcy's mother shot him a sour look. "Don't you mention that woman's name in my presence."

"Last year, you said you met your first wife when you were in Spain on a secret mission for the CIA," Carly pointed out.

"And two years before that, you said it was in Africa, while you were shutting down an illegal poaching operation," said Jess.

Marcy's father gave a good-natured shrug. "Yes, well, I've led a full life. When you're as old as I am, it's hard to keep the details straight."

Marcy's brother-in-law Earl drained the last of the wine from his glass—his *third* glass, Marcy couldn't help but note, and with dinner not even half over. He leaned clear across the table, almost knocking over the gravy boat, to give the devil a jolly pat on the back. "I hope you have a *devil* of a time tonight," he said in a too-loud voice. His boozy breath wafted across the table to Marcy as he gave the devil a broad wink. "Our family can throw a *hell* of a party." He burst into raucous laughter, looking around the table as if expecting everyone else to join him. No one did.

Marcy leaned over to tug at his sleeve. "For Pete's sake, Earl, sit down." She hissed into her husband Ralph's ear, "Get your brother under control."

Ralph shook his head sharply. "Huh? What is it, dear?" He blinked out at the table through his thick glasses. "The gang's all here, I see. It sure is nice to see everyone tonight. Now, what were we talking about? Your first wife, was it?" He nodded to Marcy's father.

Marcy struggled not to groan aloud. She never should have married an academic. It turned out the absent-minded-professor stereotype was less of an exaggeration than an understatement. "Did you see who our daughter brought home for Christmas?" She murmured in his ear.

He blinked owlishly at the devil, who smiled in response. "Glad you brought a friend along, Jess," he said. "And one with intact earlobes, this time." Then he leaned back in his chair. His eyes defocused. No doubt he was calculating equations in his head.

It looked like managing this crew was up to Marcy, just like it always was. She took a deep breath. "I'm glad to see you looking out for people who need it," she told Jess. "I've always admired your big heart. But..." She let her breath out through her teeth. "Maybe the two of us should talk privately."

Jess scowled. "Anything you have to say, you can say in front of everyone. *Including* my friend." She patted the devil's hand.

"All right, then," said Marcy doubtfully. "Jess, honey... surely you can see how bringing the literal devil home on *Christmas* is a problem for obvious reasons. For one thing, how is he supposed to go to church with us this evening?"

"Oh, I don't have a problem with church," the devil assured her. "Despite popular opinion, I won't catch fire if I walk through the doors."

His safety hadn't been Marcy's primary concern. She could only imagine the pastor's reaction when he saw their guest. "Maybe with concealer and a wide-brimmed hat..." She eyed the devil's cherry-red complexion. "A *lot* of concealer. I wonder if the drugstore is open tonight."

Jess shot her a look like she had kicked a puppy. "When I saw him looking all lonesome on campus," she said, "the two of us got to talking. He's really lonely, you know? Everyone hates the devil, especially this time of year."

"Hey, it's not like I can blame them," the devil said affably. "Source of all evil, and all that."

"I *told* him he'd have a place here," Jess said, still glaring at Marcy. "I told him that at our house, Christmas is about being able to come home and be accepted no matter who you are. I've always got a place at our table, no matter how much of a screwup I am."

"Hey," Marcy objected. "Don't talk about yourself that way. You're a bit of a late bloomer, that's all."

Jess rolled her eyes. "And no one tells Carly to get lost, even though she's an obnoxious overachiever. Uncle Earl still gets invited every year, even though he's a drunk and we all know he grabbed your boob over pumpkin pie three years ago. Grandma doesn't have any nice things to say about anyone, and Grandpa has never told a true story in his life. And as for Dad, he's too busy floating off in the clouds to see what's in front of his face."

Everyone at the table was glaring at Jess now. Everyone except for the devil, who leaned back in his chair, hands laced behind his head, like he was enjoying the show. Jess either didn't notice or didn't care. "And you, Mom," she said, "you're so busy taking care of everyone, and making sure they all get along, that you pretend you can't see any of that. And you know what? It works. Because it means we all have a place here at your table. We can all feel like we belong somewhere."

She rose to her feet, scraping her chair along the hardwood floor with a ferocity that made Marcy wince. "And don't you think everyone deserves that? I mean, if this bunch deserves it, anyone does."

"Doesn't the devil have, um, a home of his own?" Marcy ventured faintly.

"Plane of eternal torment," said the devil with a wry tilt of his chin. "Not the coziest place to spend the holidays. And besides, everyone down there is extra-cranky this time of year. I try not to go home for Christmas if I can help it."

Against her will, Marcy thought back to her own family's Christmas dinners, back when she was a little younger than Jess. Back when she had been the foul-mouthed good-for-nothing failure who had dropped out of college and came back home once a year to rub her parents' noses in the fact that she would never amount to anything. Or at least that was how her parents had seen it. Her kids didn't know about that part of her life. They would never have believed her if she had told them.

Back then, it just just been her and her parents around the dinner table. Her mom would pick at her relentlessly, pointing out every flaw and seeking out every last insecurity like a heat-seeking missile. Her dad would escape into jokes and stories, the more elaborate the better. But they always set a place for her at the table, regardless. Even the year when she swore she wasn't coming, and showed up at the last minute when dinner should have been over hours ago. And the reason she had kept going back—the reason she had gone that year she had sworn she wouldn't—was because of exactly what Jess was saying. Because she had known there would always be a place for her, even if it wasn't the most comfortable place. That was why she worked so hard to create that place at her own table now.

She shot a halfhearted glare at Jess. Now that her younger daughter had brought up *those* memories—however unwittingly—she could hardly send their guest away now. Even if he *was* the devil, and it *was* Christmas.

She would have to pray extra hard in church tonight, that was all.

She shot the devil a stern look. "Can I trust you to refrain from causing mischief around my dinner table?"

The devil shot her a crooked smile. "You really shouldn't trust any promise I make, you know. Father of Lies, and all that. But for what it's worth, I'll do my best."

She narrowed her eyes at him, then nodded. "All right," she said. "You can stay. But I am *not* taking him to church," she added with a look in Jess's direction.

"I'll handle the dishes while you're gone," the devil offered.

An awkward silence came over the table. Marcy struggled to fill it before either of her parents could—or worse, Earl. "So," she said to the devil, "what are you hoping to do with yourself once you're out of school?"

He shrugged. "Well, dragging souls to eternal damnation is a full-time job. But I've been considering getting into filmmaking as a hobby. Or maybe I'll launch a tech startup. I've got an idea for a mobile game."

Carly turned to him with a look on her face that said a lecture was coming on. "You really ought to focus on just one thing," she said. "That's how all the great success stories of the world do it. If you split your focus, you cut your available resources in half." She shot a glance at Jess. "That's a lesson my sister could stand to learn."

Jess opened her mouth. Before she could answer, Marcy's mother jumped in. "In my day, people had respectable careers," she said around her mouthful of mashed potatoes. "You didn't have every average Joe in the world running around trying to get famous. They were satisfied with a steady job in a factory or an office." She let out a long sniff. "And dragging souls to eternal damnation—what kind of made-up job is that? Do you even have an official title?"

"Prince of Darkness, ma'am," the devil said with a respectful nod. Then, to Marcy, "These are some fine mashed potatoes."

"I've known a few princes in my time," Marcy's father volunteered. "The Prince of Morocco swore a blood oath with me after I saved him from an assassin. Swore we'd be brothers until the end of time. Which I guess makes me an honorary prince myself."

Earl, deep into his fourth glass of wine, made a sweeping arm gesture that almost knocked the green bean casserole clear off the table. "Princes are overrated," he slurred. "The ladies don't want stuck-up royalty. They want a down-to-earth man, one who knows how to show them a good time." He gave Marcy a good-natured leer, then leaned across the table to wrap an arm around the devil's shoulders. "You and I, we'll go out on the town some night. I'll give you some tips."

Marcy poked Ralph's shoulder. "Take the wine away before your brother has any more, dear."

"Hmm?" Ralph blinked. "Yes, dear, the mashed potatoes are very good this year." He sank back into his chair, already lost in the clouds once more.

Marcy sat back in her own chair and looked around the table, asking herself—not for the first time—why she put herself through this every year. But she didn't have to spend too much time on the question. She already knew the answer.

She smiled and held out the bowl of mashed potatoes to the devil. "Seconds?"

THE
UNLIKABLE ONES

Bex smiled as she tilted back and forth on her wobbly desk chair. It needed replacing—had probably needed replacing ten years ago—but that would never happen. Still, she would rather have this than the fancy ergonomic chair she would have been using in the kind of job her parents had expected her to get, something that involved copying numbers from one spreadsheet to another.

She wouldn't have needed a sweater, either, because the heating system in her high-rise office would have worked all the time instead of approximately half, and the window would have locked properly. She hadn't told her parents about the unreliable heat. Her brief description of the job had horrified them enough without her needing to go into detail. Instead, she had gone out and bought a collection of sweaters—a small collection, taking the size of her new salary into account, but still enough to have one for every day of the week. It had been good timing, because the Christmas sweaters had just come out. Today's choice had a fuzzy snowman on the front, so soft and puffy she kept reaching down to touch it.

The door behind the desk creaked open, and Deirdre stalked out. She gave Bex a once-over, her eyes lingering on the sweater, and gave the snowman a sour glare. Bex didn't see how Deirdre had any room to judge. She was wearing the ugliest plaid suit Bex had ever seen. Bex sometimes thought Deirdre chose her clothes with the sole purpose of looking as dull and humorless as possible. Not to mention unfashionable. Not that Bex was a fashion plate herself, sitting here in her snowman sweater, but at least she had a sense of humor about it.

Deirdre turned her glare on Bex. "Do you need to have that thing running?" She demanded.

For a second, Bex had no idea what she was talking about. Then she followed the jab of Deirdre's pointer finger to the air freshener plugged into the outlet across the room. When she had gone to buy the sweaters, she had found a pack containing an assortment of holiday scents. It had seemed like the perfect thing to bring some much-needed cheer to the front room of the Santa's Sleigh building, with its scuffed carpet and peeling paint. Today's scent was "Gingerbread Cookie," and it smelled exactly like its namesake.

Bex shrugged. "I thought it would help make this place a little nicer."

Deirdre scowled, like she took the insult to the building personally. Which was hardly fair, because Bex had heard her complaining about the new building to

Justin just the other day, telling him they would have had just as much space and a lot more warmth if they had operated out of her own basement instead. "It smells like a bakery out here." From the sound of Deirdre's voice, that wasn't supposed to be a good thing.

"I'm the one who's out here all day." Deirdre spent her workdays in the back, at the computer she had wedged into the corner of the back room where Justin sorted all the donations. Apparently, last year he'd had a whole team of "elves"—he had actually called them that, which Bex secretly loved—to handle the actual sorting, while he stood back and directed. This year, he was doing it all himself, an elderly Santa Claus doing all the heavy lifting without any extra pairs of hands to help him.

Bex had heard Deirdre gripe at him that he should be the one out front instead, to save his joints. Deirdre didn't have any conversational mode besides griping, so far as Bex could tell. But this time, Bex privately agreed. But in the week she had worked here, she had already learned enough about Justin to know his shyness would never allow him to handle the pickups. And this was his operation, so he got to divide the labor however he saw fit. Whether it was good for his joints or not.

Santa's Sleigh was a three-person operation these days, after an unexpected fall flood had forced them permanently out of their former headquarters and made them drop everyone's pay. The employees who hadn't been let go had quit when they had seen the size of their new paychecks—everyone except Deirdre, of all people—leaving Santa's Sleigh short-staffed just in time for the holiday season. Bex privately and guiltily considered it wonderful timing, because it had opened up the perfect job for her at just the right time.

"Pickups start today," said Deirdre, interrupting Bex's train of thought. This time, she jabbed her finger at the calendar on the wall—specifically at today, December 12th. Two weeks before Christmas. As if Bex could have forgotten. "People will be coming through here all day." She gave the air freshener another sour look.

"And I'm sure they could all use a dose of holiday cheer." Bex drew in a deep breath, trying to figure out what Deirdre objected to. The smell brought an involuntary smile to her face.

"Do what you want," said Deirdre, her voice heavy with judgment. She grabbed a cup of coffee from the counter along the side wall, then disappeared out back again, slamming the door behind her.

Bex was glad Deirdre was gone when, a moment later, the front door jingled open. The reindeer bells on the doorknob had been her addition, which had drawn another scowl from Deirdre. Whoever was here, they didn't need Deirdre's scowl to be their first impression of the place.

She looked up at the clock. This had to be the first pickup, just in time. When Santa's Sleigh had chosen their recipients from the sea of applicants, through some arcane algorithm of Deirdre's—which seemed all wrong to Bex, because this seemed like exactly the kind of thing that required a human touch—they had also scheduled times for every family to come pick up their box. That way, nobody had to worry about running into somebody who would know they couldn't afford Christmas on their own. Even though anyone else coming through here would be in the same boat.

The woman who walked in was wrapped in a winter coat that looked strangely thick and bulky around the chest. A second later, Bex realized it wasn't the coat—the woman had a baby under there, snuggled against her chest in a carrier. A newborn, by the look of it—the baby still had that wrinkly-faced alien look.

The woman blinked at Bex with raccoon eyes, the dark circles so pronounced they looked bruised. She smiled. "It smells delicious in here."

Bex knew it was petty to feel so vindicated by that, but she couldn't help it. "You're Maranda Carmichael?"

The woman nodded. Her smile faded, and she didn't quite meet Bex's eyes. Justin had warned Bex about that—that nobody wanted to come here, because nobody wanted to need what they were offering. That they wouldn't necessarily be as full of smiles and effusive gratitude as Bex might expect. She had shrugged it off. She hadn't taken the job to hear people thank her. She just wanted to do some good.

Miranda's box was on the floor beside the desk, waiting. Christmas in a Box, they called it. Three wrapped presents, one for each of the woman's children—including the baby, since she had marked down on her application that she was pregnant. Deirdre's algorithm had picked the gifts from this year's donations based on the children's ages and interests, although Bex supposed the baby was too young to be interested in much of anything. The box also contained all the nonperishable foods the family would need for a simple Christmas dinner, plus a gift card that would cover a roast at the local grocery store. Justin had said they used to throw in a small gift for the adults, too, as a surprise, but of course that hadn't been an option this year. The way Justin told it, they were lucky they were still in business at all.

Miranda followed Bex's gaze to the box. She didn't move. A second later, Bex blushed, remembering the baby. She shoved her chair back from her desk and hefted the box into her arms. She started to hold it out to Miranda, then felt her face prickle with embarrassment again as she realized how absurd that was. "Here," she said, already starting for the door. "Let me take this out to your car."

They walked out of the parking lot together. The car Miranda led her to was on its last legs, with a hand-sized splotch of rust near the back wheel and the bumper hanging by a thread. Through the window, Bex could see a spot where a large chunk of plastic had snapped off the side of the car seat.

Bex's Christmas mood had stayed firmly intact since she had started the job, regardless of all the scowls and snide comments Deirdre had the sent her way. But that car seat... that dimmed the warmth in her heart, just a little. She still remembered when her younger brother had been born, and all the drama that had ensued when her aunt had tried to insist on giving them her old car seat. It had been like new, but her aunt had already used it with Bex's youngest cousin for a couple of years, and that meant it didn't qualify as safe, no matter what her aunt thought.

She could give these people Christmas in a box. They would open presents on Christmas morning, and that evening they would eat a roast and a pie and powdered mashed potatoes. But on December 26th, that baby would still be driving around in an unsafe car seat.

Justin had also warned her about that part—that no

matter what she did, she would always feel like it wasn't enough. She had shrugged that off, too. The way she saw it, even doing a little was better than nothing. But looking at that car seat, she thought she understood what he had been getting it.

Miranda opened the passenger seat for her, and Bex set the box down. She expected the woman to awkwardly nod and drive off. Instead, Miranda smiled— a genuine smile, albeit an exhausted one. "Thank you so much," she said, every bit as effusively as Justin had told Bex not to expect. "I was so afraid I wasn't going to be able to do Christmas for my kids this year, and they still believe in Santa, so I didn't know what I was going to tell them. That's why I couldn't bring them with me today. I had to ask my mom to watch them, which seemed ridiculous for a fifteen-minute trip across town, but I need those gifts to show up under the tree on Christmas morning and not a moment before. We do reindeer sounds on the roof and everything—my husband gets up there on a ladder and taps it with a toy hammer." She blushed. "I'm sorry. I'm rambling. It's just... it's been a hard year."

Bex's heart clenched. "It's okay," she assured Miranda, more fervently than she meant to. She wanted to give this woman the long talk she plainly craved. She wanted to give her a babysitter, and a better car seat, and everything she needed that wouldn't fit in one measly cardboard box.

All of a sudden, an image flashed into her mind. "Wait here," she said, and ran back into the building, almost slipping on the remaining patch of ice from last week's storm. She hurtled through the inner door and into the back room.

19

Justin had a line of cardboard boxes in front of him, and was taking cans of cherry pie filling off a stack and putting one in each box. Deirdre, as usual, was bent over her computer. As Bex burst into the room, they both looked up in alarm.

"Don't mind me," she gasped out. "Nothing's wrong. I just need this." She grabbed a tiny blue hat off the top of the pile of unsorted donations in the corner. She remembered the hat, because when it had come in, she had tried and failed to imagine a head small enough to wear it. Now that she had seen Miranda Carmichael's baby, it wasn't so hard to imagine anymore.

Deirdre glared. "What are you doing with that?"

"Bex, wait," said Justin, the corners of his mouth turning down as he looked from her to Deirdre.

She didn't wait. She took off with the hat and ran back out to the parking lot. She dodged the ice this time, and stopped in front of Miranda, panting and out of breath. Miranda took in her breathlessness, and her disheveled appearance, and her eyes widened in surprise or alarm.

Bex thrust the hat out toward her. "Here. Take this. I know it's not much, but..." When Miranda didn't take the hat, Bex reached out and awkwardly tried to slip it over the baby's head.

Miranda frowned at first, like she didn't understand what Bex was trying to do. Then her eyes misted over. "Thank you," she said quietly as she plucked the hat gently from Bex's fingers. With an expert touch, she tucked it over the baby's tiny ears. The baby grunted and stirred, but didn't wake up.

Then a hand reached over Bex's shoulder to snatch the hat away.

Bex turned. Deirdre was standing behind her, scowling.

Bex tried to process what had just happened, but she wasn't sure she could, even though she saw the hat dangling from Deirdre's fingers. "What are you doing?"

"The gifts are in their box," said Deirdre, with a jerk of her chin toward the box balanced precariously on the passenger seat. "They don't need this too." She shook the hat at Bex like the item, or Bex herself, offended her somehow.

She wasn't the only one who was offended. Snatching clothes away from a freezing baby in December—who *did* that? "It was right there on top of the pile," said Bex. "This baby could use it as much as anyone else. What can it hurt?"

"We're low on donations this year," said Deirdre, with nothing resembling human compassion in her voice. "You know that."

Miranda looked between the two of them uncertainly. "I should go."

"I'm so sorry about this," said Bex, knowing nothing she could say would be enough to make up for the shock of Deirdre's rudeness.

"It's all right," said Miranda, still looking a little stunned. Bex couldn't blame her. "Thank you again. For everything." She hastily ducked into her car and drove off.

As her car disappeared from the parking lot, Bex whirled on Deirdre. "How could you do that?"

"We still have boxes to fill." Deirdre didn't even sound apologetic. "That family already received their allotment of gifts."

"I thought the Grinch was just a story, but here she

is, standing right in front of me. Working for a Christmas charity, of all things." Bex shook her head. "Why do you even work here if you hate it so much?"

"My job is my business," Deirdre snapped. "Focus on your own. Hand out boxes and smile, and try not to screw anything up. Again." She curled her fingers around the tiny hat and clutched it to her heart as she marched inside.

* * *

When Bex got back inside, the air freshener was gone. She found it in the trashcan, broken in two. She didn't bother trying to plug it back in; one look at it was enough to tell her it was a lost cause.

According to Justin, Deirdre had been working for Santa's Sleigh for twenty years. Why would someone who hated Christmas, who hated *helping,* work for a place like this? It wasn't for the pay, that was for sure.

She tried to put Deirdre out of her mind, and studiously avoided the woman's gaze as she went out back for the next box. She sat back down behind the desk, missing the smell of cookies already, and braced herself for the next pickup. Even without taking Deirdre's drama into account, she didn't know how she was going to make it to Christmas if they were all going to be as heartwrenching as that.

But the next one, it turned out, was surprisingly easy—a man who came in stinking of beer and snatched up his box without a smile or a word of acknowledgment. Next was a woman who came in complaining nonstop about how she had never wanted those kids in the first place, and they had grown into a bunch of ungrateful brats who didn't deserve toys anyway, and now she had to lower herself to accept charity for them because her ex-husband's mother had signed them up behind her back. Bex had to fight to keep her smile up for that one. But at least neither of those two made her heart hurt at not being able to do more for them. Not like Miranda Carmichael and her baby.

It wasn't as if she didn't care about the other two. As they disappeared out the door, she wondered—with a distant sadness—what would happen to them after Christmas was over. She wondered, especially, about that woman's children. But it was a cerebral sort of sadness, just one more reminder that bad things were happening everywhere in the world. It was nothing like seeing that tiny baby curled against its mother's chest.

By lunchtime, she was feeling stronger. She had gained a little of her distance back. Maybe she could make it through to Christmas after all.

Deirdre went out to get subs for the three of them at Happy Jack's, as usual. A few minutes later, Justin came out, rubbing his aching hands. When Deirdre came back, he warmed them gratefully against the white takeout bag. Bex opened the bag eagerly, mouth watering in anticipation. But there were only two subs inside. Even before she unwrapped them, she already knew what she would find. Justin's usual barbecue chicken, and Deirdre's Italian. No sign of Bex's meatball sub.

Bex tried not to frown. It wasn't as if Santa's Sleigh had agreed to provide her lunch every day when they had hired her. She had no problem paying for her own. But she hadn't had to do that since she had started.

Deirdre had picked up lunch for all three of them every day, and hadn't allowed any arguments. It was the only nice thing she had ever seen the woman do.

Bex silently handed out the subs, and tried to pretend she hadn't noticed there wasn't one for her. The sharp look in Justin's eyes told her he had noticed too, but he didn't say anything either. He only shot Deirdre a look she pretended not to see.

When Deirdre leaned against the wall and started eating, Justin wordlessly held half his sub out to Bex. She wanted to refuse, but her growling stomach didn't let her. She thanked him, folded her hand around the warm bun, and took a grateful bite.

Deirdre saw, and frowned. "No one can resist a ray of sunshine like you," she said with a roll of her eyes.

"I didn't ask him to share," Bex pointed out.

That only prompted another eye roll from Deirdre. "Of course you didn't."

Justin silently patted Bex's arm. She shot him a questioning look—yes, she knew Justin didn't like confrontation, but he didn't seem the slightest bit surprised by Deirdre's behavior. Although she supposed he wouldn't be, if she really had worked for him for twenty years. But if that were the case, she thought she at least deserved an explanation. In answer to her silent question, Justin sent back a look of warm reassurance, which wasn't what she had been looking for.

She took the hint and ate her lunch in silence. Normally she loved what Deirdre brought back from Happy Jack's, although she had never heard of the place before coming to work here. Today, the sub tasted greasy and bland. And the atmosphere didn't improve her mood. The gingerbread smell was already fading, and without it, the room felt small and shabby. The heater hadn't kicked on in a couple of hours, and her sweater was thinner than she had thought when she had bought it.

When Deirdre finished her lunch, she pushed herself up from the wall and walked toward the inner door in silence. This was Bex's last chance to say something. But before she could figure out how to begin a conversation like that without sounding petty, Deirdre had disappeared through the door.

She didn't say anything that night, either, when Deirdre left without her usual sour nod of goodbye. On the drive home, she tried to tell herself she was looking forward to going back tomorrow and doing more good in the world. Now that the pickups had started, their hard work was finally bearing fruit. But all she could imagine was going back into that cold room, without even a warm Christmas smell to cheer her up, and handing out boxes to more people like the beer-smelling man and the woman who hated her kids. All while Deirdre acted out a grudge against her for the crime of trying to go above and beyond for somebody.

Over the drone of the radio, she heard her parents' voices telling her she had always known it was a bad idea to choose a job using her heart instead of her head. For a second, she thought maybe they were right. Deirdre was the one who had real experience with this kind of work, and if she still believed they were making a difference, why would it have turned her so nasty? What would Bex look like at the end of twenty years?

Then Bex took a deep breath and made a sharp U-turn. Honks followed her as she weaved into the parking lot of the dollar store. She marched inside like a soldier on a mission and went straight for their picked-over table of Christmas decorations. She saw what she was looking for almost immediately. And just like that, she felt a little warmer.

The next day, she came in early, this time wearing a sweater with two reindeer kissing. The first thing she did, after shrugging off her coat, was to place her purchase in the center of the desk. It was a snow globe, as big as her hand, showing Santa and all nine reindeer and a sleigh piled high with gifts. She sat, and turned the snow globe upside down, and watched as the snow drifted down onto Santa's head.

The front door opened, and Deirdre walked in. Right away, her eyes went to the snow globe.

Bex tried to call up the resolve that had come over her last night, and smiled at the woman. Deirdre didn't return the smile.

Bex felt her own smile falter. "Santa's sleigh," she said, with an unnecessary gesture toward the snow globe. "Get it?"

Without a word, Deirdre picked up the globe and dropped it into the trash. It landed with a thunk. Bex's heart clenched, but when she peered into the trashcan, the globe was still intact.

Bex wasn't smiling anymore. She glared up at Deirdre. "What was that for?"

Deirdre didn't say a word. She hung up her coat and started toward the inner door.

Bex blocked her path. "That was mine. I bought it for myself." It had only been a dollar, but it was the principle of the thing. Come to think of it, she had bought that air freshener, too. Deirdre could have simply unplugged it without throwing it away.

"Take it out of the trash if you want," said Deirdre with a shrug. "But I don't want it here. This isn't a kindergarten; we're adults with a job to do. We don't need decorations." She gave Bex a slow once-over. "Or childish sweaters."

She reached for the doorknob. Bex didn't move. "This is because of the hat, isn't it? Because I had the audacity to do more than my job required. If that's how you feel, why try to help anyone at all? Why not go be a lawyer like your parents probably wanted, and make a million dollars getting white-collar criminals off on technicalities, because screw everyone else, right?"

"The Santa's Sleigh system is designed for fairness," said Deirdre. "You interfered with that system."

Bex fought the urge to check under Deirdre's skin for circuits. "If you care so much about fairness, what about the way you're treating me?"

Deirdre gave up on trying to get through the door. She took a step back and turned her full attention on Bex. "You're right," she said, although there was no contrition in her words. "I'm not being fair to you. You know why? Because I don't like you. Tell me, how do you feel about that?"

Bex's jaw fell open. It took her a moment to collect herself enough to speak. "To be perfectly honest? I don't like you much either. You're cold and you're heartless. This job has sucked all the compassion right out of you. You should have left a long time ago."

"And stepped aside for somebody like you?" Deirdre sneered. "So you can help every cute baby who makes your heart ache?"

"Why not? If that's not the reason we're here, then what is?"

A deep, cold anger flared in Deirdre's eyes. The intensity of it sent a chill through Bex. She tried to take a step back, but her back was already to the door.

Then the bells on the front door jingled as the door swung open. For a second, Bex thought more time had passed than she had realized, and the first pickup of the morning was already here. She hadn't even gotten the box ready yet. She faced the door and tried to paste a smile on her face.

But Justin was the one to walk in. He took in the scene with a single glance. "It's time to get started," he said mildly, in his barely audible voice. "We're still behind. Bex, the first pickup will be here in ten minutes. Deirdre, get back to work. We had a few last-minute applications come in, and we need to match them to the unassigned donations we still have."

Bex stepped to the side and slid back behind the desk. Deirdre disappeared through the inner door.

But Justin didn't follow her. "Bex," he said. "Go out to lunch with me today."

Bex glanced toward the door. She could barely hear Justin; her head was still full of Deirdre's words. "You've known her a long time, right? Why does she work here? Why do you let her *work* here? She's clearly miserable. And she's making everyone else miserable along with her."

"Lunch," Justin repeated. "Today. We'll talk."

She knew, from what she had picked up on, that it took a lot for Justin to set foot in a place full of people he didn't know. If he was willing to suggest it himself, this had to be serious. So she dropped the questions and nodded.

He flashed her a barely-there smile and disappeared

into the back room behind Deirdre. Before she had a chance to gather her thoughts, the front door opened again—the first pickup, here ten minutes early. The second the chubby-cheeked toddler waddled into the room behind his mother, asking if it was true that this was Santa's workshop, she knew this would be another one to make her heart ache. But that was okay. Better that than for her to turn bitter like Deirdre.

* * *

Justin must have said something to Deirdre about their lunch plans, because she didn't come out at noon to make her usual Happy Jack's run. Instead, Justin came out in her place. He slipped on his coat and motioned to Bex.

Bex walked out the door after him. "She's mad that you're taking me to lunch, isn't she?" she asked, as she picked her way across the parking lot, mindful of the ice.

"What makes you say that?" Justin asked.

"She isn't even going out to get her own lunch. Instead, she's sitting and sulking and working through her lunch hour."

"Deirdre would work through every meal if she could," said Justin, with a private smile that spoke of long familiarity. "She only buys lunch for us because I feel shaky if I don't eat something. She goes out every day because she knows how hard it is for me."

Bex tried to reconcile that with the Deirdre she had seen so far. "She does that for you, but she doesn't want me to help the people you're paying us to help?"

Justin opened his mouth, then seemed to think better

29

of it. "Let's go someplace where it's easier to talk," he suggested. "It's a little cold out here."

They got into Justin's old beater of a car and drove five minutes to Happy Jack's. Bex had never actually seen the place before now. She had imagined a cold, cramped room squeezed into the middle of a strip mall, with just a counter and a couple of plastic tables. Instead, the building stood on its own, squat and homey with warm wood siding. The interior was spacious, with dark wood booths and pleasant amber lighting. A Christmas tree sat in the corner, draped with green and gold lights.

Justin tensed as he looked out at the room, where a couple of people stood in line at the counter and a few more were eating quietly. "I'll order," he said. "You sit down." He faced the counter and took a long breath.

Bex shook her head. "I'll do it."

Justin placed a gentle hand on hers, just for a second. "It's my fault we're here in the first place. I should have explained Deirdre to you from the start. It's been so long since we've had a new person come to work for us, it's easy to forget that not everyone knows her like I do. So the least I can do is buy you a lunch." He strode up to the counter before she could object.

She chose a booth and waited. In a moment, he came back with his usual and hers—not on a tray like she had expected, but on real plates. She could see how shaken the brief experience had left him, and his shoulders stayed hunched around his ears, but she didn't comment.

He saw the way she was looking at him, though, and smiled wryly. "We've all got our stuff. I'm lucky to have found a place where mine doesn't get in my way. I can stay in the back sorting donations, and know I'm making people every bit as happy as if I were talking to them face to face."

"And Deirdre?" Bex wanted to eat, if only to make Justin feel like his efforts had been worthwhile, but Deirdre's words from this morning were still sitting in her stomach like a lead weight.

"You're wrong about her not caring," he said, although his voice remained gentle. "She revolutionized Santa's Sleigh, you know. It was dying when she came on board. We had a bad reputation—too many people in need, not enough to offer them. And most people wanted to donate to the bigger organizations, anyway. I didn't go looking for Deirdre—she came to me. She told me had ideas for how to turn us into a real contender in the charity sphere again, and even said she would accept half pay until those ideas panned out. I accepted. I didn't think she could do it, but she did."

"And those ideas had a lot to do with efficiency," Bex guessed.

Justin answered with a nod and a soft smile.

"I already know she cares about efficiency," said Bex. "That's not a surprise. But does she care about the people we're supposed to be helping? Does she understand that there are faces behind those anonymous numbers on her computer?"

"Better than you know." Justin's eyes had a faraway look. "I don't know if you know how long Santa's Sleigh has been around. But it's an institution around here, every bit as much as the DMV or the Post Office, even if for a while there it had the reputation of the former more than the latter." He laughed quietly to himself. "I started it up when I was still young and idealistic." At that, he gave her a significant look that made her squirm the same way she did when an elderly relative told her she looked just like her mother had at her age. "I never expected it to endure as long as it has."

"Deirdre," Bex reminded him, before he could drift too far into memory.

Justin nodded. "Yes, Deirdre. Her family was on our list for a few years, when she was a child. We did things differently back then. I would hire someone to dress up like Santa—I could never get up the nerve to do it myself—and we'd have a big party. Families in need would come, mostly parents with young children, and Santa would hand out presents. Then everyone would have a big dinner together. It wasn't as private as it is now, but it was cheerier. I spent most of the time in the back room, but I always listened by the door. I loved hearing the sounds of happy children. But I didn't make the connection that Deirdre had been one of them until she told me, three full years after she started working for me." At that, his expression turned troubled. "Of course, she wasn't one of those happy children, not really."

"What do you mean?" Bex asked.

"Deirdre has always been..." His lips tilted up in a half-smile. "I suppose the best way to say it is that she was born without the gene that lets a person shrug and go with the flow. She's a contrary one—always has been. You can either fight it, or learn to love her for it."

Bex frowned. "Being contrary is one thing. Being mean is another."

Justin opened his mouth to speak, then shook his head and began again. "Every year, I had more people than I could handle competing for the Santa job.

32

Everyone loved looking the kids in the eye and seeing their big smiles. That mattered to them more than the money did. But Deirdre didn't smile easily, even when she was happy. And when she did... well, she was never a cute kid. Definitely not the chubby-cheeked cherub people imagined when they took the job. And people are a lot shallower than they like to believe they are. So Deirdre watched, year after year, as all the good presents went home with the kids who were easy to like, and she got whatever was left."

"So now she wants to take out her resentment from decades ago on people who weren't even alive then?" Bex didn't know why Justin had thought this explanation would help anything.

"You misunderstand," said Justin. "She's not taking anything out on anybody. Deirdre just wants everything to be fair. Back then, she didn't see the big fun party the rest of us saw. What she saw were people who were easier to love and easier to drum up sympathy for, getting the best of everything—the toys, the smiles, the attention—while people like her got scraps."

"Maybe she couldn't help her face," said Bex, "but she could have learned to be a little nicer."

"She could have," Justin allowed. "Maybe. But that's never been who Deirdre is. And as she grew up, she saw a lot of other people who weren't like that either. People who never seemed to get any extra help from people like you who pride themselves on going above and beyond." Justin shook his head. "Places like Santa's Sleigh always have less than we need. That's a cold, hard fact. Especially now, after the flood, and with donations declining a little more every year. If you give a hat to a baby because you feel sorry for her and her mother, some other baby goes without."

Against her will, Bex pictured the woman who had complained about her children, and the man who stank of alcohol. Her face flushed.

"She hates this time of year," said Justin with a small sigh. "It always reminds her of those parties. But she also loves it, deep down, because she can do for other people what no one ever did for her. Her algorithm is all about numbers. It keeps things fair. No smiles and cute faces to sway people. You don't know whether the person on the other end of the screen is someone you'd love or someone you'd hate, and she likes it that way. She believes in it enough that she's willing to endure the judgment of people like you, who don't see things the way she does."

He let out a longer sigh and picked at the bun of his sandwich.

"But like I said, we all have our stuff," he said. "That's why she's been treating you the way she has. You radiate that well-meaning idealism that wronged her so badly, way back then. When you gave the baby that hat, all she could imagine was the baby who wouldn't get one. The one who wasn't cute enough, or was crying too loudly for you to feel sorry for them. She was imagining herself, out in the cold with nothing to keep her head warm." He met Bex's eyes with a weary gaze that seemed to go straight through her. "I talked with her this morning. She can't go snatching things away from the people we're here to help. She can't be throwing away your belongings, either. But it's important for you to know where she's coming from. And what she's trying to do."

Bex didn't say anything. She wasn't sure what Justin wanted to hear, or what she wanted to say.

"You're still thinking you don't like her much," said Justin without breaking their gaze, "aren't you?"

Bex dropped her eyes with a blush.

Justin chuckled. "It's okay. Not many people do." His laughter softened into a smile. "That's kind of the point."

* * *

When they went back to the office after lunch, there was still no sign of Deirdre. But if Bex closed her eyes and listened, she could hear the clacking of her fingers on the keyboard. Deirdre was still here; she was just keeping herself hidden away. Sure enough, when Bex went in for the next box, Deirdre was hunched over her computer, pretending not to notice her.

She didn't say anything to Deirdre. She grabbed the box and brought out front with her. Then, remembering, she reached down and pulled the snow globe out of the trash. She plunked it down defiantly on the desk. She was watching the snow settle at the bottom when the next pickup walked in.

As soon as the woman entered the room, Bex knew this would be an easy one. The woman was wreathed in an aura of cigarette smoke that made Bex fight to suppress a cough. She had a flat look in her eyes, like she had stopped caring about anyone and anything a long time ago. "Is this where I pick up the charity box?" she asked as she approached the desk. Her voice was sharp and demanding, and rough from decades of smoking.

A girl of about five or six trailed behind her, her face

twisted in a parody of a spoiled pout. She kicked the leg of the desk, almost causing the snow globe to topple over. "I don't want other people's smelly used toys."

The girl's mother didn't chastise her, or even look her way. She hefted the box into her arms without a word of thanks to Bex.

The girl kicked the desk harder. "This place smells like Santa farts." Bex placed a hand over the snow globe just in time to keep the kick from knocking it over.

Balancing the box in her arms, the woman strode away without a glance behind her, like she had forgotten she was supposed to have a child with her. The girl gave the desk a third kick, then rushed after her mother. Bex felt no twinge in her heart as she watched them go. Not like she had when Miranda Carmichael had driven out of the parking lot.

Was this what Deirdre had objected to? People like her not wanting to stick their necks out for people like these? Sure, she felt bad for whatever Deirdre had gone through, but was she really supposed to feel sorry for that brat?

Without meaning to, she watched as the girl chased her mother out the door like she was afraid she would actually be left behind. She had a sudden flash of a child in pain, ignored, her whole body suffused with embarrassment at getting her Christmas toys from this place instead of having Santa come down her chimney like everyone else.

On a sudden impulse, she grabbed the snow globe and rushed after them. "Hey, wait!"

The mother turned around sluggishly, faint annoyance breaking through her aggressive air of apathy.

Bex bent down and held the snow globe out to the girl. "I want you to have this."

"Why?" the girl asked crossly, folding her arms across her chest.

Bex quashed her impulse to take it back, go inside, and declare herself done with this whole experiment. She forced her face into a smile. "Because it's not used and smelly." She leaned in, like she had a secret to tell. "I bought it yesterday, and I've been waiting all day for the right person to give it to. That's you."

The girl blinked at her. Her arms fell heavily back to her sides. "Really?"

Bex nodded. "Yep."

The girl's mother stared at her, brow slightly furrowed, like she didn't understand what was happening. "Hey, thanks."

The girl waited another few seconds, like she thought Bex might change her mind. Then she snatched the globe from Bex's hands and stared raptly at the Santa inside as she followed her mother back to their car.

Maybe Bex had chosen her sweater more wisely that day. Or maybe the heat had finally started working. But when she went back inside, she actually felt a little warmer.

That day, after work, she didn't go back to the dollar store. She went to the nicest of the three department stores instead, the one she'd had to give up once she got a look at her new salary. She filled her cart with small and mundane items, the kind of things that made a person feel warm inside—literally or metaphorically. Scarves, coffee mugs, stuffed animals. A few bigger things, too, like a half-off winter coat that still cost more than she should be spending.

It was a dumb impulse, she knew, just like she already knew she would regret it when January came around. But someday she would be old and bitter like Deirdre. Or, hopefully, old and wise like Justin. Either way, she would know better than to spend her entire salary on gifts for strangers. So the way she saw it, she might as well take advantage of all the time she had left to be young and stupid before she gained that kind of wisdom.

Not a one of these things would make it anywhere near the donation pile, so Deirdre wouldn't be able to complain about her using up their limited resources. Although she suspected that when Deirdre saw who she planned to give all this out to, she wouldn't have a word of complaint.

When the cart was full, and she knew the contents would strain her bank account as much as it could bear and then some, she started toward the checkout. Then, as one last thought occurred to her, she made a sharp turn toward the greeting card aisle. She browsed until she found the cheesiest card in the store, with an angry reindeer biting the rear of Santa's pants and pulling them down to reveal a thong underneath. There. Now she had everything she needed.

When she got home, she wrote a message inside the card, in blocky, anonymous capitals. *THANK YOU FOR MAKING THE WORLD A FAIRER PLACE. YOU'RE MAKING A DIFFERENCE.* She didn't sign it.

She went in early the next day and left the card on Deirdre's keyboard. Then she sat at her desk and read the paper until the others came in. When she went out back for her first box, Deirdre was trying to maintain her usual dour expression as she bent over her computer. But when Bex looked closely, she could see Deirdre's lips tilting upward in the slightest hint of a smile.

Broken Wings and Christmas Things

If Tori's roommate subjected her to one more schmaltzy holiday movie that took place in a cutesy coffee shop, Tori was going to vomit. Better yet, she would drive across the country to Hollywood just to dump hot coffee in the lap of whoever wrote it. Even better, she would tie them up in her trunk with the glittery tinsel hanging over the counter that tickled her nose every time she walked past it, stick a Choosy Brews apron on them, and make them work a shift. Five minutes in this place would be enough to cure them of their romantic delusions. Ten minutes, and their next holiday movie would be in the vein of a Tarantino film. Tori would watch that.

There were no meet-cutes happening here, and no picturesque flurries of snow drifting by outside the window. Only customers too illiterate to realize they had walked straight past two Starbuckses—or was Starbucks both the singular and the plural?—in their trudge through the yellow-brown slush on the way here, just so they could get angry when Choosy Brews didn't have the exact same seasonal drinks that were on the Starbucks menu. It didn't help that when Tori had to explain their mistake to them—in a voice as sweet as a Choosy Brews candy-cane mocha, and without using the words "illiterate" or "blind as a bat," because the customer was always right—she was contractually forbidden from mentioning any of their competitors, including *that* one, by name. As well as saying the names of any menu items said competitors might offer. Someone up in management at the parent location two states away, in a town where Starbucks had never taken hold and they probably never even had this problem, was overly paranoid about lawsuits.

Tori had thought the January blues weren't supposed to start until, well, January. That was when everyone was worn out from two straight weeks of parties, bad-tempered from being back at work, and perpetually hangry thanks to their New Year's diets. But it was still two days until Christmas, and the customer crankiness level had already gone up several notches. Half the customers had started their diets early. Tori could tell by the way they defensively justified ordering their coffee with cream and sugar by telling her how little they had eaten for breakfast—*Three strawberries and a half-cup of granola with milk, skim milk of course*—as if the local barista doubled as the food police. The other half was hungover from the aforementioned parties. And everyone was either exhausted from their shopping, or stressed out by the prospect of braving the picked-clean stores to hunt for gifts at the last minute, or both.

That combination meant everyone was fresh out of holiday cheer by the time they stopped in at Choosy Brews for their morning Starbucks specialty drink. Because yes, they all wanted the seasonal specialties. And not a single one of them was satisfied by the drinks Choosy Brews actually offered. Which was unfair of them, because even as coffeed-out as Tori was, even she had to admit the candy-cane mocha was a tiny piece of heaven in a cup. Even if she never wanted to hear the words "candy cane," or anything else associated with this benighted holiday, as long as she lived.

The customer who was stomping out the door right now—one of the dieters *and* hungover, which was a toxic combination—had wrinkled her nose when Tori had suggested giving it a try. She had demanded some kind of caramel-mint concoction, a combination that sounded nausea-inducing to Tori. The next couple in line hadn't realized it was their turn yet. They were busy arguing about whether to break up now or stay together for another week so they wouldn't have to explain a breakup to their families over the holidays. Watching them sneer at each other, Tori couldn't imagine how they thought they were going to con anyone into believing they were a happy couple for five seconds, let alone an entire week.

The customers who already had their coffee didn't look like the dose of caffeine was making them any happier. A man in a suit sat at a table, scowling at his phone and periodically jabbing out a message. A couple of young teens had told their families they were somewhere else—Tori could tell by the way they kept laughing nervously and glancing furtively out the window. She gave it another half-hour, at most, before one of their parents stalked in here to drag them out. If Tori was lucky, she wouldn't get an earful from said parent about being an accomplice to their delinquency.

While she waited for the couple to forget they hated each other long enough to remember they were still standing in line, Tori glanced out the window past the truant teens, wondering how long it would be before she had that angry parent's alcohol-and-skim-milk breath in her face. Because of course they wouldn't cut her a break, not two days before Christmas, no. Not when everyone's nerves were frayed past the breaking point with plans and pressure and unwanted relatives. Tori was up for eating the rich as much as the next underpaid barista, but she had to admit, Scrooge had had a point.

But there were no angry feet marching up to the door yet. At this moment, there was no one on the sidewalk at all, potential customers or otherwise. Just half-melted piles of puke-yellow angel poo. That was what Tori's little brother used to call snow, mostly because of the way it had made Tori shriek. Tori hadn't appreciated his sense of humor back then. Working at Choosy Brews was good for that much—she had finally shed enough of her romanticism to appreciate the potty humor of a six-year-old.

Wait. Tory squinted. There was something strange out by the fire hydrant on the other side of the street, something crumpled and sunken half into the snow. It was white and fluffy, like a fancy fur coat. But dotted with speckles of red. Read that, at least from this distance, reminded her uncomfortably of blood.

Not my problem, she reminded herself. She was just

here to pour coffee and get yelled at. Anyway, it probably only looked like blood to her because of how morbid this time of year made her. It was probably confetti, or tinsel, or something else suitably festive.

A gust of wind ruffled the coat, revealing pale flesh underneath.

Tori had thought the past couple of weeks had killed had killed any empathy she might once have possessed. Apparently not, because just as the argument couple remembered where they were and stepped up to the counter, she called, "I'm going on my break," and pulled off her apron. As the two halves of the couple opened their mouths simultaneously, united in their outrage, she turned her back on them, threw on her coat, and rushed out the door.

She darted across the street, not bothering to go the rest of the way up the block to the crosswalk. She stooped next to the fire hydrant. Closer up, what she had thought was fur was actually feathers. Feathers? Who walked around in a feather boa these days, even during the holidays?

She didn't linger on the question, though, because those speckles of red were definitely blood. And there was a figure lying underneath, facedown in the snow, with his limbs twisted at odd angles.

Tori reached out a hand, but stopped short of actually touching him. She seemed to remember something from a first-aid class saying you shouldn't touch someone who was injured because you could end up hurting them worse. She didn't know whether that still applied if they were likely to die of frostbite otherwise. "Hey," she said softly. "Are you okay?"

She tried to keep the fear out of her voice. She had to

be calm about this, professional, even though her heart sped up with every second that went by without a response. Whatever was wrong with this guy, a panicked barista fluttering over him wouldn't improve his day any.

Although there was probably nothing much wrong with him. He had gone to one holiday party to many, and on the way home he tripped and fell and passed out from the alcohol, and cut himself on the fire hydrant on his way down. A little cut, his arm or his leg, nothing serious. He would show her, after he woke up, and she would laugh at herself for getting so worked up over nothing. Not to mention possibly sacrificing her job. At that thought, her humanitarian mood soured, which at least had the side effect of easing her nerves a bit.

He still hadn't answered her. She raised her voice. "Do you need help?"

Nothing.

Great. That was just what she needed today—to call an ambulance and wait around for them to get here, while she was supposed to be working. How long was the ambulance response time around here, anyway? Probably longer than her fifteen-minute break. And her manager was probably already getting an earful from the angry couple. She glanced across the street at the Choosy Brews sign. If she was quick, she could get back over there in time to make nice with her manager and salvage her job.

But the man in the snow still wasn't moving.

Tory sighed in resignation. "I'm going to call an ambulance, okay?" She placed a hand on his back, because there was no way a touch that light could do any damage, and she needed to wake him if she could.

As soon as she touched the feathers, she froze.

It wasn't a feather boa. It was *wings*. Growing straight out of the man's back. She ran her finger over the bony protrusions, just to be sure. It wasn't a costume—or if it was, it was professional-level work, not the kind of thing someone in sad little Wildeview wore to their drunken holiday parties. The man had wings growing out of his back, and the reason she had seen bare flesh underneath was that he was stark naked. He definitely hadn't gone to any holiday parties *that* way, no matter how drunk he had been.

Just like that, she knew what she was looking at, although it took her another few seconds to admit it to herself. There was a dead angel lying in the snow across the street from Choosy Brews.

What exactly was she supposed to do about that? They hadn't taught her this one back in elementary school when they had drilled her and her classmates on emergency numbers. Did 911 handle nonhumans? Maybe she should call a priest instead. Did any of the local churches have an emergency hotline?

The wing under Tori's hand twitched. Tori jerked back. When she was done with her almost-heart-attack, she leaned down over him, listening for the sound of breathing. "Hey, are you..." *Alive?* "...okay?"

The angel turned his head to look her in the eye. That small movement was enough to draw a groan of pain from him. He had a gash above his eye, dripping dark red blood. Not enough blood to be responsible for the red on his wings. She wondered where the rest of his injuries were, and how serious. But his bright blue eyes were alive and aware.

"I..." The angel's voice was weak with pain, but

underneath, it was dark and rich. "I wish to make a bargain with you."

She shifted closer to him before she realized what she was doing. That voice was like a fresh-brewed candy-cane mocha, but with a whole lot less sweet. She realized she had stopped hearing the traffic sounds for a second—stopped hearing anything but his voice, and then the echo of his voice—and shook her head to clear it.

"I need a quiet place to rest until I heal," the angel continued. "If you provide me what I need, I will bestow upon you wealth beyond your imagination."

That broke the spell a bit, if only because it wasn't what she had expected to hear. Not that she knew *what,* exactly, she had expected to hear. Tidings of comfort and joy, maybe. She gave the figure another once-over, just to make sure he really was what she thought he was. "Wealth beyond your imagination" didn't sound like a very angelic thing to promise. Maybe she had only thought *angel* because her mind was still on the dirty snow and her brother's stupid joke.

But there was really nothing else he could be. She hadn't been to church since middle school, but she still knew what an angel looked like.

The angel must have seen her hesitation, because his torn-open brow creased in a worried frown. "Perhaps you would prefer it if I doubled your lifespan instead?" he offered.

Tori cleared her throat. "Not that they aren't both tempting offers," she said, "but aren't you supposed to be asking me to help you out of the goodness of my heart? Or, I don't know, because you're on some important mission for all of humanity?"

The angel's face twisted in a sneer. For a second, Tori couldn't help but think of the arguing couple back at Choosy Brews. "There is no goodness in the human heart," he hissed. His voice wasn't sweet anymore. It was bitter and mean, and still somehow compelling. It reminded her of the best black coffee she had ever tasted. "Only avarice. But I can feed that avarice, if it suits your purposes." His voice was chocolatey-rich now. "What is your heart's desire, human? I can fulfill it for you, and for such a small price."

Okay, he definitely wasn't here to spread holiday cheer. His voice wasn't working its magic on Tori anymore, because he had tipped his hand too far. He wanted her to trust him. He wanted her to bargain with him for things like a doubled lifespan and wealth beyond imagining, in exchange for her giving him practically nothing in return. Because *those* stories always ended well.

The angel tried to sit up, and collapsed back onto the snow with another, louder groan. "Well, human?" The effect of his demanding tone was spoiled by the pain in his voice and the fact that he had a mouthful of snow.

Tori took a longer look at him. At that cut above his eye, to be specific. And the hints of all-over bruises his change in position had revealed. And how one of his wings was twisted at an odd angle, probably broken. She hadn't noticed that at first; she had been too preoccupied with the fact that he had wings at all.

"How did you get those injuries?" she asked, in a voice every bit as demanding as his.

The angel's eyes darkened. "That is not your concern. Will you accept my deal, or—"

Tori crossed her arms in front of her chest as she

interrupted him. "Did you fall from heaven?"

The angel flinched. Only for a second, but Tori saw it. "You need not concern yourself with such questions. I can offer you anything you—"

"You can just stop right there. You're a fallen angel, and you're trying to trick me." Strangely enough, her nerves were gone now. Maybe because the part of her that had been afraid was also the part of her that didn't believe in angels.

"There are no tricks here. Anything I promise, I can deliver."

Tori met his coaxing gaze with a glare. "Maybe that's true, but I wasn't born yesterday. There are always strings attached." She gave Choosy Brews another glance. Her break had to be almost over by now. "Look, I don't have time for this. I'm supposed to be at work. So why don't you go tempt someone else?"

The angel reached out for her as she stood up. "No! Wait." There was no fresh-brewed smoothness in his voice this time. It was probably the first genuine thing he had said since Tori had gotten here.

Tori didn't crouch down again, but she didn't walk away, either.

"I... did not expect a literal fall," the angel admitted through gritted teeth. He sounded angry, but not at her—or, she thought, even at the fall itself. More like he was angry that he had to show this much vulnerability in front of one of the humans he held in such contempt.

Which didn't exactly make Tori any more inclined to stick around. Why should she listen to someone who not only wanted to trick her into some kind of devil's bargain, but didn't bother to show how little he thought of her while he was doing it? "And this is my problem why?"

"My injuries will heal, given time," the angel said. "But I need to find a more secluded place to recover before any other humans see me. I know what they would do to me if they saw me as I am now, in my true form. They would pin me like a butterfly, and stick me in one of their zoos. My powers are... greatly diminished, at the moment..." Another grimace. It took him a few seconds to force out the rest of the words. "And I do not know if I would be able to stop them." He paused. "I can, of course, deliver on any promise I make to you. After I am recovered."

Maybe he could, maybe he couldn't, but Tori didn't particularly care one way or the other. Not that a few extra decades of life didn't sound nice. And to be honest, limitless wealth sounded even better. It would mean no more shifts at Choosy Brews, for one. But she had read enough fairy tales as a kid to know that anything that looked too good to be true probably was. She would rather work at Choosy Brews for the rest of her life than spend her life looking over her shoulder, wondering when the bill was going to come due.

"I've never seen a zoo with an angel exhibit," Tori said doubtfully. "But even if someone did try to do all that, why not just bribe them the way you're trying to bribe me?"

"You seemed sufficiently..." He paused, visibly searching for the right word. "Vulnerable. I have no guarantee that I will be as lucky with the next human who notices me."

How flattering. Tori tried to stand a little straighter. "You don't have a very high opinion of humanity, do you? Either we're weak and naive suckers, or we're sociopaths who want to stick you in a zoo."

The angel responded with another sneer. "I have watched your kind, *served* your kind, for thousands of years. I have seen firsthand all the terrible things you do to one another. I endured it as long as I could, but at last I decided I could no longer serve such cruel and selfish creatures." He swallowed, then winced in pain. "Others found this decision... unacceptable. Which led me to my current state."

Sympathizing with the fallen angel was probably the first step toward letting him tempt her into that bargain of his. Still, she couldn't help but think maybe he had made the right call. In this holiday season alone, she had seen enough of humanity to be right there with him.

Even so, his words made her bristle. Because hadn't she come rushing out here to see if he was okay? And risked losing her job to do it? And it wasn't as if she had known he was going to offer her a reward. She had done it out of the goodness of her heart, as much as he had sneered at the notion.

But standing here in the cold being offended wasn't doing anything for her except making it less likely that she would get her job back. Since she wasn't going to take his offer, she might as well leave him here to fend for himself. If he thought no humans had enough kindness in their hearts to help him, she might as well prove him right. He probably *was* right. Look at her, more concerned about her crappy job than the bleeding man in front of her. Although he *was* inherently evil, if she remembered her Sunday-school lessons correctly, which had to change the equation a bit.

"I will not make the offer again, human," said the angel, not bothering to hide the sneer underneath his words this time. "Anything your heart desires, in exchange for a private place to recover until I am healed. Will you accept?"

"Last chance. Right." Tori scoffed. "It's not like you're in any position to make threats. Your offer will be open for as long as I'm standing here, because if I leave, you'll be at the mercy of whoever comes along next." She could have just said no, but she was still mad about that comment of his. Did he even know how much her rent was? Or how hard it would be to find another job that paid even the pittance she was getting from Choosy Brews? Until he knew what she had risked by coming out here to dig him out of the snow, he could keep his mouth shut.

Anger flared in the angel's eyes. But when it passed, the sadness underneath was enough to make her feel a tiny bit guilty. It wasn't as if he had just woken up one day and decided to hate humanity. If he was telling her the truth, it had taken him thousands of years to get to the point of falling. He had probably spent a good portion of that time caring about humanity enough to wish for them to be better.

But if all he had seen in those thousands of years was a parade of cruelty and misery, he hadn't looked closely enough. There were plenty of good things he could have seen if he hadn't been so determined to prove his own beliefs true. Like someone rushing away from a job they needed at the sight of a bloody fur coat in the snow. Like an exhausted parent leaving work to track their errant teenager down and cart them home. Like two people who had fallen out of love, but were willing to drag out their own misery to make their family celebrations a little happier for everyone else.

"The answer is no," said Tori. "I don't want what you can give me."

"I can give you anything. Name your price." The look in his eyes had gone from coaxing to desperate.

Tori looked across the street, then down at his sneer and his bloody wings, and made a decision. "Here's what I want. I want you to come home with me and rest for as long as you need to. No bargain, no cost, no strings attached. I want you to see that humans aren't as bad as you think we are."

His eyes widened; the sneer faded. She had caught him off guard. He shook his head, wincing at the motion. "No human would do such a thing and ask nothing in return. There is always a cost—and hidden costs are always the most painful to pay."

"Funny, that's exactly what I told you—or don't you remember? But I'm not hiding anything. I already told you the cost. You have to let me break your worldview by showing you that humans are capable of doing something nice for someone else every once in a while. Is that too high a price for you?" Well, if it was, at least she wouldn't lose her job. But the more times she looked at the Choosy Brews sign, the less certain she was that she cared. She could find something else—not as good, probably, but something. The angel, though... he might not.

He hesitated, and for a moment she thought she was right—it really was too high a price for him. But then he clutched the fire hydrant with both hands and pulled himself up to his feet. His bruises were even worse than she thought, and now that she could see him properly, she no longer had to wonder where all the blood had come from. The only question was which of the half a dozen gashes was responsible.

He tried to pull his wings around himself, but the broken one wouldn't move, and the other one didn't do much to cover anything. And even if it had worked, it wasn't as if wrapping himself in his own wings was going to make people stare any less than walking down the street naked. Between the injuries, the nudity, and the wings themselves, he was going to get looks no matter what he did.

Tori took off her coat and draped it over his shoulders. He was taller and broader than her, and the wings were too long to hide completely. But the coat covered all but the lower tips of the wings, which would be enough to minimize the stares, and it did an even better job of hiding everything else once she pulled it closed. The buttons looked like they would pop any minute, but they held. She wasn't sure how she would get the bloodstains out, but she could always just buy a new one with all the money she wouldn't be making.

He looked down at the coat like he thought it might eat him. An unexpected rush of affection for him swept over her. It was probably dangerous to go all mother-hen over a fallen angel, but she could worry about that later. After she figured out how to explain him to her roommate.

Without a word, she offered him an arm to lean on. After a second of hesitation, he took it. They hobbled down the street together at his slow pace, and Tori didn't look over her shoulder at Choosy Brews once. She was definitely going to lose her job, which was a disaster in more ways than she wanted to think about right now, but maybe it would at least mean she could watch one of those stupid coffee-shop movies without wanting to barf. She wondered if the angel was up for a holiday movie.

No Warm Fuzzies

Eddie leaned back against the brick of the storefront behind him, shifting so the cold of the sidewalk seeped into a different part of his bottom. He gave a small, happy sigh as he gazed out at the scene across the street. A toy store had their Christmas Eve display out. Yes, the store had multiple Christmas displays—one for December first, one for the week before Christmas, one for Christmas Eve, and one for Christmas Day itself. He'd been coming to this corner for years, and he had always thought the Christmas Eve display was the most beautiful, with a column of animatronic deer pulling Santa's sleigh, raising and lowering their hooves in the relentless rhythm of a march. Soft red and white lights blinked like a bloody snowfall.

Below the window, at the edge of the curb, lay a dead raccoon. It hadn't been content with rummaging through garbage cans on that side of the street—it had thought the grass was greener over here where he was. And it had paid the price. Its intestines lay splayed out in the street in thick red loops. Its eyes bulged out from its misshapen head, like it was boggling at the enormity of its own mistake.

He took a breath of the crisp winter air. Beautiful, all of it.

He jangled his hat at the young couple passing by. "Spare a dollar on Christmas Eve?"

The man took a break from whispering sweet nothings in his sweetheart here to sneer down at him. "Get a job!" he called as they passed.

Eddie only smiled up at him in response. The smile was because it was Christmas Eve, and nothing could bring his mood down with such a beautiful view in front of him. It was also because he knew how little effort it would take him to kill that man and his sweetheart both, if he had the mind to. He would kill the woman first, he thought. Make the man watch. The man wouldn't have much to sneer about then.

But he didn't do that kind of thing anymore. It was a pleasant daydream, nothing more. He watched them pass and got his hat ready for the next passersby.

"Hey!" a young woman called from a few feet down the sidewalk.

The heat in her voice made him look up. The smile on his face grew. One more beautiful view on this blessed day. She was cute in a fresh-faced farm-girl way, her round cheeks ruddy from the cold, her long blond hair tied back in a braid. She was dressed for the season, all in red and white, and her red jacket had little poodles dressed like reindeer trotting along the bottom.

Her appearance didn't match the anger in her tone.

He almost asked what he had done to her besides sit here, but he didn't—if she wanted him to know, he would find out soon enough. And it turned out he wasn't talking to him, anyway. She planted herself in the path of the young couple, making them stop and look at her with identical frowns.

She put her hands on her hips. "What's wrong with you?" she demanded of the man. "This man is a veteran! He served our country!"

Eddie frowned. How had she known that?

"And it's Christmas Eve!" she continued, her face getting redder with every word. "You can't spare a single dollar? On Christmas Eve? Even if you're that much of a Scrooge, you could at least have the decency to keep your opinions to yourself!"

"Thank you," Eddie said to the woman with a nod, "but I don't need your help. Let this gentleman go on his way."

"You heard the man," said the man, and shoved his way past the angry farm girl, dragging his sweetheart behind him.

The farm girl walked up to him, face still flushed. "I'm sorry about those idiots."

"Unless you sent them here, I don't see what you have to apologize for." He looked closer into her face. "To what do I owe the pleasure? It's not every day a stranger comes along to defend me. Or do I know you?"

The more he looked at her, the more certain he was that he did not, in fact, know her. No big surprise—he didn't know much of anyone these days. He sure would have liked to get to know her better, though. At least if he had been a couple of decades younger. He could just imagine what his younger self would have liked to do to her. Red blood on a red jacket. Rivulets of the stuff matting that long blond hair. It would have been a sight more beautiful than the toy store display and the dead raccoon put together.

A pity he wasn't that man anymore. But he wasn't too old to dream. He leaned back and drank in the sight of her.

"The shelter sent me to check on you," she said. "I'm a new volunteer. They say you like to come out here on Christmas Eve and look at the display."

"They had it right," he said. "I'm fine. You can go back and tell them that."

But she didn't move. "It's getting late. You'll want to head back to the shelter before dark, or there might not be a bed for you."

"There are never enough beds on Christmas Eve," he agreed. "It's a cruel time of year. Tensions are running high. People getting kicked out of their homes, or running away and finding themselves with nowhere to go. Plus, everyone is strapped for cash from buying gifts they can't afford, so they're less willing to give someone a break on rent." He shook his head. "So much for Christmas charity. Anyway, that's why I'm out here. To make room for the ones who aren't used to being out on the streets."

"It's going to be below freezing tonight."

"I expect so," he said. "Last I heard, we might even be in for a white Christmas. A lot of children will wake up happy tomorrow morning. But don't you worry about me. I can handle the cold for one night. I'm used to rough conditions."

"That's not right," she said, with an intensity that

made him wonder if this was the first injustice she had ever encountered in her short life. "There should be room for you at the shelter. You shouldn't have to sleep out in the cold. You served our country! You deserve better!"

"And the kid who just got kicked out of the house on Christmas Eve doesn't?" He shot her a crooked smile. "It's all right, I promise. I can take care of myself."

She shook her head. "I can't just leave you out here. It's Christmas Eve!" She bit her lip, thinking. "I'll tell you what—I'll take you out for dinner. Then you'll at least have something warm in your belly."

"I can't imagine the shelter sent you out here with money in your pocket to buy an old man dinner," said Eddie. "And if they did, that's a poor use of funds on their part. They should be saving up for a bigger building, so they don't run into this problem next year."

"They didn't," she said. "But my Christmas bonus came in, and—"

He held up a hand. "And nothing. You go spend that money on a gift for yourself. Or donate it to the shelter. It won't be the first time I've scrounged up dinner for myself in the cold."

"If you're going to sleep outside on Christmas Eve, of all nights, you should at least get *something* good beforehand," she insisted.

Eddie sighed to himself. His enjoyment at the sight of her was quickly turning into a gnawing irritation. "Don't do this," he said wearily.

"Don't do what? Try to help a man who deserves better than what he's been given?"

"Don't try to give yourself some warm fuzzies and pretend you're doing it for me. I've been living this life a long time now. I know all about people like you. People who tell themselves they're doing something to help the less fortunate, but really they just want to make themselves happy. If you want to make yourself happy, take that Christmas bonus and buy yourself a fancy dinner for one. You'll be able to afford twice as much wine without a second person at the table, and you won't need to make me a prop in your little inner drama."

She didn't get mad, which was a shame. She only looked at him with fresh pity in her eyes. "I know you've probably seen a lot in your life to make you lose faith in humanity," she said, her voice newly gentle. "But some people really are here to help. I promise." She leaned over and laid a soft hand on his upper arm.

He jerked back like she had burned him. "You don't want to do that," he said, a warning note in his voice.

"I'm sorry," she said hastily, straightening up and pulling her hand back. "I didn't mean to scare you."

He laughed. He rarely laughed these days, and when he did, it was an ugly sound. "Scare me? No. You're the one who should be scared. You want to know what I did in the war? I got information from prisoners. Anyone they couldn't make talk, they sent them to me. I always got what they were looking for, no matter how many bones I had to break along the way. The more the better, as far as I was concerned."

She still didn't leave. And she still had that look of pity in her eyes. "You did what you had to do," she said. "But it's over now. You can forgive yourself. If you're trying to punish yourself by depriving yourself of a warm bed to sleep in, or a nice hot meal to celebrate the holiday, you don't have to do that. I'm sure you've been punished enough. It's okay to let go."

The pleasant haze of his fantasies was long gone now. His hands clenched at his sides. He wished he had something sharp to twirl between his fingers, so he could imagine plunging it into her soft flesh. "I didn't do what I had to do," he said. "I did what I *wanted* to do. The only reason I joined the military in the first place was because I wanted a place where I could kill without getting locked up for it. You ever hear about those kids who torture cats and set fires? Well, that was me. The only difference is, I was smart enough not to get caught. And to figure out I'd get my face on the ten o'clock news eventually if I didn't find myself another outlet—and I didn't have any interest in spending the rest of my life locked up. I value my freedom."

The military hadn't been as satisfying as he had imagined it would be. At least not at first. In the army, you kill from a distance. You don't get the satisfaction of plunging a blade into flesh. You don't get to see the life leave your victim's eyes.

But it didn't take long for some canny individuals to figure out his skills and offer him a chance to make use of them. Hell, they'd probably seen people like him before. No doubt they recognized the look in his eyes. And once they'd given him a chance to shine... he let out his breath in a long sigh. God, he missed it. If not for his bum leg, he'd still be there now.

The farm girl took a step back. Her eyes were wide. She blinked too fast. The flush in her cheeks was of a slightly different color now. Not outrage, or a simple flush from the cold. She was afraid. He could smell it on her. He'd always been able to smell fear. It was the sweetest scent there was. Better by far than any of those flowery potions women liked to douse themselves in.

He brought his hands up where she could see them. "I always was good with a knife," he said. "I don't have one these days, though. Haven't in a long time. I don't trust myself with it, see. Some people would say I'm stupid for sleeping out here without a weapon for protection, especially since I'm getting up there in years." He tightened his hands into fists and loosened them again, slowly and deliberately, for her benefit. "But just because I like a good blade doesn't mean I need one. Some of my most memorable moments don't involve anything more than me and my own two hands, and someone who doesn't understand how much I can do with those hands until it's too late."

She took another step back.

He gave her a toothy smile. "Careful there," he said. "You're getting close to the curb. Don't want to stumble out into traffic. Might want to get a look at what happened to the raccoon who tried it before you. He's right behind you."

The color in her cheeks disappeared, turning her face unnaturally pale. Her gaze darted to one end of the block, then the other. He saw her calculating whether she had the chance to run before he struck.

He sighed to himself. Oh, hell. Fun as it was to make the fear roll off her in waves, there was no call for him to be playing with this do-gooder like she was a mouse and he was the cat who had her caught between his paws. Not on Christmas Eve.

"I was just having a bit of fun with you," he said. "I'm not going to hurt you. I don't do that anymore. If there's one thing the military is good for, it's teaching discipline and self-control. And I still value my freedom.

I've got a good life these days, full of simple pleasures. I can get a hot meal at the shelter when I need it, and a bed to sleep in most nights. And during the day, I've got nothing to do but see the sights." He motioned to the Christmas display behind her. "And I'm getting old. I've got no interest in living out the rest of my days in prison."

She locked her eyes on him, watching him as warily as a gazelle might watch a nearby lion. She didn't run. Whether he had reassured her at all, or whether she was simply frozen in fear, he couldn't tell.

"Besides," he added, "it'd be a shame to kill a sweet woman like you just to make myself a bit happier for a few minutes. Especially when I've already got plenty to keep me happy that doesn't involve hurting anyone else. Like those Christmas lights in that window." He sighed, louder this time. "Even if you are an obnoxious do-gooder," he added, half to himself.

A little of the color came back into her cheeks. She glanced down the road again, and he thought he would finally be rid of her. But then she did what he didn't expect. She took a step closer and fixed him with a stern glare that made him feel like he was back in Sister Clara's third-grade class all over again.

"You want to scare me off, huh?" she demanded. "Well, that's too bad. If you're dead set on sleeping out in the cold this Christmas Eve, fine. But I'm going to give you a merry Christmas before I leave you to the dark and the cold, whether you like it or not." She crossed her arms, and frowned, and did everything but stamp her foot.

"If you're hoping for a Christmas movie, there's plenty playing on TV," he said. "If you won't rest until you find some selfish way to feel like you're doing a good deed, fine. Give me some of that Christmas bonus of yours and let's call it a day." He held out his hat. "But don't tell yourself it's about me. You'll be buying yourself some of those warm fuzzies you want so badly, that's all."

"I am *going* to give you a bit of happiness on Christmas Eve," she said through her teeth, "and you are going to let me."

"Why me? Why not go to the shelter and pick on someone who actually wants what you have to offer?"

"There are plenty of people out there to help those poor kids who got kicked out of their homes on Christmas Eve," she said. "At the very least, they've got warm beds to sleep in, thanks to you. But who's going to help someone with your history? No one, at least not once you tell them what you told me. And that's not right. Christmas is about helping *everyone*. Not just the cute little Tiny Tims of the world." Her eyes glowed with a fierce light that scared the objections right out of his mouth. "I'm not going anywhere until I find a way to give you a bit of happiness. If a nice hot dinner isn't your thing, fine—what do you like?"

"Pretty girls," he told her, his eyes locked on hers. "Especially their eyes bulge out as my thumbs dig into their soft, supple necks."

She rolled her eyes at him. "Still trying to scare me off? Well, I've got bad news for you—it's not going to work."

"You're not afraid I'm going to drag you into an alley and show you what I mean? Because maybe you should be." He tightened and loosened his fist, where he was sure she could see it.

65

She rolled her eyes. "If you were going to do that, you wouldn't tell me beforehand. Besides, you already said you weren't going to hurt me."

"I could always change my mind. Or maybe I was lying to make you let your guard down."

"You don't want me to let my guard down. You want me to leave you alone. Well, guess what—that's not going to happen. If you want to get rid of me, the quickest way to do it is to tell me what you want to do tonight, so we can get on with it."

"Maybe I want to see what shade of red those cheeks of yours turn as the life drains from your body," he said. But his heart wasn't in it anymore.

She could tell, too. He knew because she lifted her chin in subtle triumph. "So, what do you say? Pet some dogs at the animal shelter? Go ice skating in the park? Do you like to read? We can go to the bookstore, pick out a few new books for those long, boring nights."

How long had it been since he'd owned a book of his own? He'd long since worn out the only ones in the library that interested him. But he wouldn't give her the satisfaction of showing a lick of interest.

Too late—her eyes lit up. "You like books, huh?" she held out her hand to him. "The nearest bookstore is only a few blocks away. Come on, let's go."

"I know where it is," he muttered. "But I can't go there. Not tonight. They'd take one look at me and kick me out."

She frowned in curiosity. "Why tonight? If they're going to kick anyone out—and they shouldn't, because reading is for everyone—Christmas Eve would hardly be the night to do it."

He shook his head at her innocence. If she really

thought everyone in the world was as filled with the Christmas spirit as she was, she was in for a rude awakening. "They're having some fancy-pants poetry reading tonight," he said, staring down at his lap, hoping he wouldn't reveal too much. "I wouldn't make it two steps inside before someone showed me the door."

"Poetry? Like a Christmas thing? *The Night Before Christmas,* and all that?"

He shook his head. "That's not poetry," he said before he could stop himself. "That's kids' stories. This is real poetry. Nakita Khensamphanh is reading from her new collection tonight."

She was silent for a long moment. In the silence, he knew he had screwed up. His suspicion was confirmed when she said, "You like poetry, don't you?"

Too late to deny it now. He shrugged as his face drew into a dark scowl. "Poet was about the only career I could ever see myself having once I got out of the military," he admitted, suddenly too bashful to look her in the eye. "Poetry is all about beauty, and you may not think it, but I have a deep appreciation for beauty. The kinds other people can see, and the kinds they can't." He nodded to the Christmas display in the toy store window, then at the raccoon in the road. "But poetry doesn't sell, and I didn't have the money for school, so I decided on of the simple life instead."

"Poetry reading it is, then," she said, with a hint of steel in her voice that told him he had better not contradict her. "I'll make sure they don't kick you out. Let's go—we don't want to be late." She held her hand out to him again.

He shook his head, even though there was a part of him—a bigger part than he was willing to admit—that wanted to take her hand. "I'm not giving you what you want tonight," he said. "No warm fuzzies. Your kind gets too much encouragement as it is. The whole world lines up to give you cheers and pats on the back for being so selfless, when the truth is, you're as selfish as the rest of us."

"Oh, so you're going to deprive yourself of something you want just because you don't like me," she said. "Fine. If that's how you want it, I'll take your advice and find someone else to give me the warm fuzzies I'm looking for, since clearly that's all I'm after."

When he snuck a look up at her, she was watching him through narrowed eyes. A blatant challenge was written across her face.

He held her gaze and didn't say anything.

She tossed her head and started walking away. "You had your chance," she said over her shoulder.

He ground his teeth. "Wait," he muttered to the sidewalk.

She stopped. When she turned around, the smile on her face didn't have any gloating in it. It was friendly enough that it almost made him want to smile back.

"You ready to go?" she asked.

"Fine," he said. "But if they kick us out, don't say I didn't warn you."

When he let her help him up, a warmth seemed to pass from her skin to his. It ran down his arm and into his gut, where it burned like the soft warmth of an old-fashioned wood stove.

Damn it. The warm fuzzies. He hadn't known they were contagious.

He scowled and pulled his hand away. "Don't get too comfortable," he said. "I still might change my mind and drag you into that dark alley."

She met his scowl with a farm-girl smile. "You're welcome."

CHRISTMAS FURLOUGH

Suriel wordlessly passed her ID through the bulletproof glass to the stern-faced seraph on the other side. She didn't know why she had to show her ID every time—she had been working here for centuries, and everyone knew her face by now, and besides, she had the wings and the halo and the angelic glow. What else would she be doing in an angelic prison besides showing up for guard duty? But they did like their security procedures around here, which meant she would be stuck showing her ID with its unflattering picture until the end of time.

The seraph squinted down at the photo, then up at her, like he thought she might be some kind of demonic spy. She rolled her eyes. "Oh, come on. No one has a disguise *that* good."

The seraph, cursed with the same lack of humor as everyone else in this prison, glowered at her. Finally, he passed the ID back and pressed the button that would unlock the door. It opened with a deep groan and a low screech of metal.

Suriel thought longingly of the crisp air outside, and the city streets aglow with Christmas cheer. Somewhere out there, children were assembling gingerbread houses and setting out cookies for Santa. Couples were ice skating in the park, and laughing as they lost their balance and fell into one another.

With a heavy sigh, she walked through the door. It slammed heavily shut behind her.

The smell of brimstone washed over her, along with the familiar air of the prison, oven-hot and oven-dry. Not for the first time, she wished she were stationed in the coldest part of hell, where Lucifer was imprisoned. Sure, there was always the risk of him breaking free, but at least it was cold there. Here in minimum security, it was nothing but minor demons and devils, and they all stank to high heaven—so to speak. And the place was always as hot as the desert—even now, on Christmas Eve, when it was cold enough to snow up above. The humans were going to have a white Christmas tonight.

Meanwhile, Suriel was going to sweat through her uniform and breathe in the stink of unwashed demon. Just like she did every night.

"You'd think an angel would get Christmas off," she muttered to herself as she walked down the dim stone hallway with its baleful red glow. "But no. We don't even get overtime pay."

Someone could at least have given this place some Christmas cheer. She had suggested putting up a string of lights, but the dirty looks she had gotten in response had made her abandon the idea. It was just as well—

there weren't any outlets down here for her to plug them into. But a wreath or a few strands of tinsel wouldn't have hurt anyone, would it?

Suriel loved Christmas. It was her favorite time of year. But the cheer up above made the gloom of the prison even harder to tolerate—and it wasn't like it was easy the rest of the year.

She did her customary cell check, peering through the bars to make sure all the prisoners in her designated area were safely locked away. Normally, she gave them a smile and a wave. Tonight, she added a, "Merry Christmas!" Mostly, she got growls and curses for her trouble. No one around here was willing to get into the holiday spirit, it seemed.

There were no lakes of fire here in minimum security. No wailing and gnashing of teeth—not unless someone decided to make one of the more recalcitrant prisoners take a shower after several stinky weeks of going without. And the prisoners around here weren't dangerous enough to require any serious vigilance. It was just a bunch of boring cells carved into the volcanic rock. It made her job easy. It also made it tedious as all get-out.

At last, with all present and accounted for, she breathed a sigh of relief. Now for her to decide how she wanted to spend the rest of her shift. The only reason she was here was because prison regulations required a certain number of guards on duty at all times. But those regulations had been written for the more dangerous parts of the prison. No one around here ever tried anything—it had been a few thousand years since they'd had a proper escape attempt. Most of the demons recognized that they had a good thing going here, even if they like to throw around a few curses to keep up appearances. Most guards brought a book to while away the time.

She hadn't brought a book in a while, though. She did have the new Grisham upstairs in her apartment, sitting by her nightstand, but she had other ways she preferred to spend her shifts these days. Speaking of which... She went to the one cell she hadn't checked yet and knocked softly on the thick stone door. "Hey," she called through the bars. "Can I come in?"

"You're a guard," Bragzoth grunted. "You can barge in whenever you like."

"That doesn't mean it's not polite to ask." She leaned against the wall and waited.

"Fine," said Bragzoth after a long moment. "Come in."

Bragzoth was lying in bed, his gnarled fingers laced behind his horned head. He had one furry leg crossed over the other, giving her a good look at his freshly waxed cloven hooves. She suppressed a smile. Bragzoth did have his vain side. It looked like he had waxed his horns while he was at it.

Bragzoth smiled when he saw her, and quickly pressed his lips together to hide it. "I knew it was your shift," he said. "I can smell the stink of angel from a mile away. And your stink is riper than most."

Suriel rolled her eyes. "As if you can smell anything over the of that fur of yours," she said agreeably.

"I'll have you know I just watched," he said with a frown. "And with the good soap, too—" Then he realized he had taken her bait, and laughed wryly at himself as he swung his legs down to the floor. "Did you bring that delightful human device again?"

By which he meant the portable gaming system she

had introduced him to. They had started off playing chess together, with an old thrift-store chessboard she had picked up, but they had soon grown familiar enough with each other's moves that they always ended in a stalemate. They had moved on to more sophisticated board games, and then games of the electronic variety. Lately, they had been playing a colorful cartoon game about zombie teddy bears.

But today Suriel shook her head. "Not this time," she said, and ignored Bragzoth's groan. "I thought it was the right occasion for something more festive." She brought a small wrapped gift out of her pocket. "Merry Christmas."

She held it out to Bragzoth. He took it gingerly, and ran a black claw along the polka-dotted paper and the shiny silver ribbon as if the gift was an artifact from another world. "Merry what?" he asked with a quizzical frown.

Suriel boggled at him. "Are you telling me you don't know Christmas?"

On second thought, maybe he wouldn't, being a demon and all. How long had he been down here, anyway? "Christmas is a human holiday," she explained. "It's... um... well, there's a religious component, but I don't think you'd like that part. The best part is the celebrations, anyway. Up there, everything is all lit up, and the humans sing beautiful songs. Everything smells sweet and fresh and a little spicy. Families come together and give gifts, and everyone smiles and hugs each other and tells all their family members how glad they are to see each other, even if they aren't. And they probably are, at least a little, because it's *Christmas*. And everything is warm and cozy, and there are crackling fires and comfy sweaters..." Suriel wrapped her arms around herself happily, wishing she were wearing a fuzzy sweater right now instead of her grim black uniform.

No sweaters for her. No family, either. Families were for humans. All she had was her small lonely apartment up in the human world, and this job down below.

Her smile fell away. Her hands dropped to her sides.

She did have a tree waiting for her. She'd decorated it and everything. It was a small one—there wasn't room for a full-size tree in her apartment—but it was still a tree. And she'd baked cookies, so everything smelled like sugar and cinnamon. It wasn't the Christmas all the humans around her got to have, but it was something.

She forced the smile back to her lips. But she wasn't feeling it anymore.

Bragzoth was still turning the gift over in his hands, like he couldn't figure out what to do with it. Suriel felt a flash of pity for him. This was probably the first Christmas gift he had ever gotten in his life. What must it be like to have never gotten a Christmas gift?

Then she frowned. Had *she* ever opened a Christmas gift? It wasn't as if she had anyone to exchange gifts with. She had watched plenty of humans open gifts, mostly on TV, but... had she ever done it herself? For that matter, had she ever *given* a gift before?

She sighed, feeling the Christmas spirit drain right out through her toes into the cold stone floor.

She sat down on the edge of the bed next to him, even though that was strictly against regulations. "Here, I'll show you how." With awkward fingers, she tugged at the ribbon. It wouldn't come loose. She must have tied it too tight—she didn't have much practice at this.

She frowned and grunted with exertion as she pulled tighter, which only made the knot more secure.

"Are you trying to get that off?" Bragzoth asked, tilting his head at her. "It looks like someone tied it like that on purpose."

"Yes, that's the point. It's a Christmas gift. You wrap it up and give it to someone. Then they unwrap it and see what's inside."

"Why go to the trouble of wrapping it up if they're just going to unwrap it?"

"Because it looks pretty. It looks like Christmas." She ran a finger along the silver ribbon. "This is what the snow looks like when it's falling in the moonlight."

"Then why do you want to take it off? Snow falling in the moonlight sounds like a good enough gift all on its own." His voice filled with quiet longing. She wondered if she had ever seen snow. Her heart ached with an answering longing. Outside, the city streets were probably dusted with white by now, and here she was sweating like it was the height of summer.

Bragzoth took a look at her face and frowned. "If you're going to be that sad about it, I'll do it."

"I'm not sad," she protested, and swiped a hand across her eyes.

Bragzoth snatched the present away. With one of his claws, he sliced cleanly through the ribbon and the wrapping paper underneath. He opened the cardboard box inside and stared down at the small pile of cookies. Some were shaped like stars, some were elves, and some were Christmas trees. She had wanted to give him more, but she hadn't had room in her pockets for a bigger box, and she wasn't allowed to bring a bag in with her. More prison regulations.

He lifted a cookie between his fingertips, and flinched when a crumb broke off onto his lap. "What are these fragile things?"

"They're cookies," she said. "You can eat them. See?" She broke off the top of a Christmas tree and popped it into her mouth. She smiled as the taste of sugar and cinnamon spread across her tongue. She had been secretly disappointed with them when she had sampled them before—they were drier than she had expected, and not sweet enough. But they tasted a lot better shared.

The demon bit a piece off a star. He made a face. "Too sweet," he announced. "And there's no substance to them. I could eat a dozen of these and not be full. Give me a good raw slab of meat any day."

Suriel tried not to be to hurt. He probably didn't know she had baked them herself, and besides, demons were hardly known for their tact. "It's not really about the taste," she tried to explain. "It's about the feeling. They taste like Christmas."

"Christmas tastes too sweet and leaves you hungry?" He held the cookie out in front of him and peered at it through narrowed eyes.

That wasn't actually a bad description, now that she thought about it. But it left out the soul of the thing. The warmth. The glow in the heart, like hunger, like longing, but a *good* longing. She looked away from the cookies to stare down at her lap. Here she was, the only angel in this place who actually enjoyed Christmas, and how absurd was that? And instead of spending her Christmas Eve wandering the snowy streets and listening to children sing carols in the park, she was spending it in this grim place with a bunch of demons who didn't even know what Christmas was.

A reckless thought came to her. She hastily pushed it away. But it wouldn't leave her alone.

It was a terrible idea. Maybe the worst idea she'd ever had in all her millennia of life. But she had never done a single reckless thing in that long lifetime, and look what it had gotten her—this job down here, and the sad apartment up above.

She watched Bragzoth from the corner of her eye. "If you had the chance to escape," she said, "do you think you'd have the strength to resist? To stay a prisoner, when it would be easy to walk away?"

Bragzoth frowned at her. "If I had the chance to escape, why wouldn't I take it?"

"What if taking it would get me in trouble?" She carefully didn't look at him.

"How much trouble?"

"The kind that would end with me stripped of my wings and sitting in a cell next to you."

"I wouldn't be next to you if I escaped, now would I?" said Bragzoth.

Of course he wasn't taking this seriously. "Never mind," she said to her lap. "I'll eat those cookies if you don't want them."

Bragzoth's face sobered. "I could never put you at risk," he said. "Not even if it meant missing out on a chance to escape. Mind you, I'd be kicking myself for the rest of eternity for not taking the chance. But you're the only one who's ever treated me well in this place. I couldn't repay you like that."

She had no way of knowing whether he was telling the truth. He was a demon, after all. But maybe that was part of living dangerously—not knowing what would happen. She had never not *known* before.

She stood and brushed cookie crumbs off on her uniform. "Come on," she said, offering him her hand. "I'm giving you a furlough."

"A what now?"

"A day off," she said impatiently. "I'm taking you up above. A simple disguise should do it. The others won't notice anything—they're all too busy with their books. It's a good thing nothing ever happens around here." She shot Bragzoth a stern look. "Do your part and don't draw attention to yourself, and we'll be fine. I think."

* * *

On an ordinary night, the city was nothing much to look at. It was small enough that most people had never heard of it, but big enough that for people living in downtown—like Suriel—the traffic noises and the acrid smell of exhaust were constant. It had no major attractions, no claims to fame. It was built entirely in shades of gray and brown, with a little black thrown in here and there.

But this was no ordinary night. Tonight, the city was dressed up like a giant Christmas cookie. The air was perfect—cold enough that a single breath sent a shot of energy through her, cold enough that her breath puffed out in front of her in tiny clouds. Snow drifted down lazily in the glow of the streetlamps to land on the sidewalks in a fluffy carpet. Holiday music and the sound of laughter drifted out of every store.

She grinned at Bragzoth, whose horns were hidden beneath a wide-brimmed hat. He had thick boots to cover up the cloven hooves. Aside from a few curls of fur escaping from under the ankles of his pants, he could have passed for human—as long as no one looked too closely at his face.

She spread her arms and left the snow drift down onto her coat sleeves. "This," she announced, "is Christmas. Isn't it beautiful?"

A car whizzed down the road, kicking up snow as it passed by. Bragzoth jumped back. "What manner of creature is that?"

"That's a car," she explained patiently. "It's not a creature at all. It's... a form of transportation. There's a human inside it, making it go. See?" She pointed to the next car, showing him the human behind the windshield.

"If you say so," Bragzoth said shakily. He pointed up at the streetlamp. "The lights, though—with so many lights burning, how is the city not on fire?" A man passed by dressed as a punk Santa Claus, and Bragzoth pressed himself up against the wall, looking nothing like a demon dangerous enough to belong in a prison— even minimum security. "What is *that?*" he asked in a near-whisper. "I've lived thousands of years, and I've never met his kind of demon before."

Suriel had planned to take him to a bar. It had seemed like a suitably demonic activity. She knew of one nearby that had a raucous Christmas celebration every year that lasted well past one in the morning. She had never gone personally, because raucous wasn't her style. Her style ran more to sitting in her sad little apartment, shivering because the heat had gone out again, and watching out the window as everyone else had a good time. When she wasn't overworking herself, that is. But she had been willing to step outside her comfort zone for the sake of introducing Bragzoth to Christmas.

Now she hastily revised her plans. Maybe they should try something more sedate.

After a moment, she took his clawed hand in hers and strode briskly down the sidewalk, pulling him with her as she kicked up snow. "Come on," she said over her shoulder. "I have something to show you."

She led him to the giant tree at the center of town. It must have been at least thirty feet tall, and was draped in enough rainbow lights to be visible from blocks away. Standing on the sidewalk looking into the park felt like standing inside a rainbow. She drew in a deep breath of appreciation.

Carolers were singing around the tree. Throughout the park, people were listening and swaying to the soft music. Suriel had never had the chance to come hear the carolers before. She had always been working.

The music thrummed in her bones, warming her like she was seated in front of a roaring fire. She basked in the feeling of togetherness. She had never really felt like she belonged in the city, seeing as everyone else here was human and she... well... wasn't. But now the fact that she had wings under her coat, and had existed since the beginning of time, hardly seemed relevant. They were enjoying the music. So was she. They were here to bask in the joy of Christmas. So was she.

Beside her, Bragzoth shifted. "I still don't understand the point of all this," he said quietly in her ear. "Why stand out in the cold to listen to music? Don't they have... what are those things you told me about? Radios? They could listen to one of those inside where it's warm."

She shook her head at him. She gestured to the tree,

then the singers. "It's beautiful," she said, with a catch in her voice. "That's the point. Even a demon should be able to understand beauty."

He squinted at the tree. "All right," he muttered. "It's pretty. I'll give you that." He wrapped his arms around himself. "But it's still cold out here. I'm not made for this kind of weather."

He didn't feel it—the warmth, the joy, the feeling of being connected with everyone else on the planet who was celebrating Christmas right now. If he did, he wouldn't have cared about the cold. "You spent... oh, I don't even know how long... alone in a cell with no one but me to keep you company," she said. "Doesn't it feel good to be out here with other people, seeing the same things they're seeing, feeling the same things they're feeling? Doesn't it feel good to be somewhere where it doesn't *matter* that you're a demon, or that you're supposed to be a prisoner?"

Bragzoth gazed out at the crowd. He drew in a long breath of appreciation. She thought she had finally reached him, until he said, "They *do* smell tasty. It's a big crowd—they probably wouldn't miss one or two, right?"

Suriel tightened her hand around his before he could get any ideas. "You promised," she reminded him.

"I promised not to run off. I never promised not to eat people."

"You are *not* eating anyone. Not on Christmas." And then, when he still hesitated, "If you do, my bosses will find out. And you know what will happen to me then."

He heaved a long sigh. "Fine," he grumbled. "I don't suppose I could just scare them a bit..."

She glared at him. "Do you want me to take you back? Or do you want to see more?"

"All right, all right," he said hastily. "I won't scare them. It really is true what they say—angels have no sense of fun whatsoever."

Suriel took a curious look at him from the corner of her eye. He sounded awfully eager for her not to take him back yet. Could it be he was getting into the spirit of things?

No, he probably just didn't want to go back to his cell yet—and who could blame him? Still, she wasn't going to give up. She would make him understand the spirit of Christmas before the night was through.

Their next stop was Birch's, the biggest department store in the city—and the most well-decorated. Suriel had mixed feelings about celebrating Christmas by shopping, although maybe her feelings would have been less mixed if she'd had anyone to buy gifts for. But either way, it wasn't really indulging in crass commercialism if they just basked in the atmosphere and didn't buy anything, right? She kept a tight hold on Bragzoth's hand—half to keep him from freaking out and running off whatever he saw someone dressed up, half to ensure he didn't go back on his word and find a tasty human to eat.

They walked through the store, threading their way through the mass of panicked last-minute shoppers. Christmas carols played on the stereo. The whole store smelled like pine—it felt like walking around inside a Christmas tree. And everywhere, there were garlands of white lights. The store had even dimmed the regular lights for the occasion, to add to the effect.

And then she did indulge in crass commercialism after all, because she couldn't resist buying a candy cane at the checkout. Everyone should experience the taste of candy cane at least once in their lives, she figured, demon or not. She handed it to him as they walked back out into the store, and tried not to wince as he bit off the entire bottom half, plastic and all.

He made an awful face and claimed not to like it. But he finished the whole thing.

Their next stop was a little theater that did nothing but play *It's a Wonderful Life* on a loop from the morning of Christmas Eve to the morning of Christmas Day. They got there just in time for the next screening. Suriel watched Bragzoth at first, while trying not to be too obvious about it. She tried not to feel too disappointed when he sat there stone-faced. And then she got too caught up in the movie to pay attention to him. She only remembered her demonic charge when the lights came up and found her swiping at her eyes.

Bragzoth was rubbing his own eyes. He looked away quick when he saw her watching him. "Must be allergic to humans," he sniffed. "It's a good thing I don't spend much time up here."

After that, Suriel figured he'd grown acclimated enough to the human world to try that bar after all. But when they got there, the place was already closing down. Suriel checked her watch in surprise. How was it that late already?

She stared out at the distant lights of the tree, feeling homesick all of a sudden, even though she couldn't think of any place she would rather be. Except maybe in the park again, listening to the carolers who had long since gone home.

"We should head back," he said. "My shift will be over soon. We can't have my replacement noticing you're missing."

"We should head back," Bragzoth agreed.

Neither of them moved.

Staying out any longer was too much of a risk. The prison always got busy around shift-change time. It would be easy for someone to notice Suriel doing something out of the ordinary.

But she had a few thousand years of risk-taking to make up for, by her estimation. And it was Christmas.

"One more thing," she said decisively. "We're going ice skating in the park."

Bragzoth looked doubtfully toward the trees. "It's quiet now," he noted. "Haven't all the humans gone home?"

"That just means more room for us."

"I thought we weren't supposed to be in a public space once it's closed for the night. That's what the owner of that bar seemed to be saying."

"If anyone catches us," Suriel pointed out, "we'll have bigger problems."

They went back to the park and climbed the locked gate. Suriel almost giggled as they hunted in the darkness for skates that would fit them. The only reason she didn't was that angels didn't giggle. But she was growing increasingly tired of only doing what angels were meant to do. After all, angels also worked the night shift in prison on Christmas.

They couldn't find any skates that would work for Bragzoth's cloven hooves. In the end, she led him out on the ice in his bare hooves. After one touch, he yelped and pulled his leg back. "It's cold!"

"Of course it's cold. It's ice. We could always go back."

"No, no. I may as well try it. If only to see what sorts

of tortures these humans have invented." He stepped gingerly out on the ice. He shivered, but didn't leap backward this time.

Suriel wobbled and clutched the railing until she found her balance. "Now slide," she urged him. "Like this." She glided across the ice to demonstrate, and promptly landed flat on her bottom.

Bragzoth looked down at her skeptically. "Like that? Are you sure?"

She laughed. The sound surprised them both. "It's not so bad," she said, trying to right herself and failing. "Just try it."

He did. To her chagrin, he had much better balance than her, and didn't look like he was in any danger of falling. She tried again, and had the same results as the first time.

Bragzoth shook his head at her, already halfway across the rink. "How is your balance so terrible?" He asked. "You have wings, for Lucifer's sake!"

"They're hidden under my coat," she groused.

"So take them out. I shouldn't be the only one freezing my extremities off."

With a token protest, she shrugged her coat off. The sting of the cold on her arms was eclipsed by the joy she felt when her wings unfurled. When was the last time she had stretched her wings outdoors? Normally, she couldn't risk it—she didn't want any humans spotting her. It went without saying that she hadn't gone flying in longer than she could remember.

Bragzoth was right—the wings did help with her balance. She caught up with him easily, then overtook him. By the time she made a full circle, her skates were barely grazing the ground.

"Hey, that's cheating!" Bragzoth protested. He raced to catch up with her. His hat flew off and landed on the ice, his horns in full view.

If anyone had been watching, they would have seen an angel and a demon laughing as they raced each other across the ice. It was a good thing it was too late for anyone to still be out—even on Christmas Eve. Everyone was safely tucked away into their beds by now, waiting for Santa Claus and the promise of a warm hearth the next morning.

Suriel spun around to face him and took both her hands in his. With a flap of her wings, she lifted them both into the air. They soared above the Christmas tree, then over the tallest buildings of the city, high enough to look down on the city like it was a snow globe. She heard a sound she didn't recognize, wild and tinkling like the way snow sounded in her dreams. She realized it was her, laughing.

And then her laughter died as she caught a glimmer of red on the horizon. Had the entire night passed already? Surely they couldn't have spent that long out on the ice. But they must have, because sunrise was coming.

And so was the change of shift.

"It's time to head back." But she didn't land yet. She made a slow, lazy circle around the city, knowing they needed to hurry but not wanting this Christmas Eve to end.

Bragzoth must have sensed the change in mood, because his face sobered. "Well, what are you waiting for? Land us already. We must be almost out of time."

But she kept flying in circles. "You really meant it," she marveled. "You're not even going to *try* to escape."

"Of course I meant it. I said I wouldn't put you in any danger, didn't I? What do you take me for?"

"Well... you *are* a demon."

"Well, I'm also your friend. So let's get back to prison already. Who's going to play games with me if you get yourself caught?"

But she kept circling.

As she did, she watched Bragzoth out of the corner of her eye. She felt a stinging at the corners of her eyes— something more than the cold. Maybe he was a demon, but he was also the only real friend she had. And she was going to send him back to prison. On *Christmas Eve*.

Before she could think better of it, she landed in front of the Christmas tree and slowly released his hands. "Go," she told him. "Get out of here. Before I change my mind."

Bragzoth didn't listen, of course. He stood there like a lump, blinking at her. "What are you doing?"

"What do you think I'm doing? I'm letting you escape. So go, already."

He stared. "You can't. You told me what would happen."

She forced a smile—and, to her surprise, found that it wasn't so forced after all. The cold made her skin tingle with excitement. It had been a long time since she'd found something worth getting excited over.

"Only if I get caught," said.

She saw him open his mouth to refuse his freedom again. Then saw him close it, because really, how many people could resist freedom that many times in a row, whether angel or demon or something else? "You want to come with me?" He finally offered, holding out a hand.

It was tempting. But she shook her head. "I'm guessing there are places you can go," she said. "Places where a fugitive demon would be welcome—and an angel wouldn't, on the run or not."

With a shrug of acknowledgment, he nodded. "Are you sure you'll be safe?"

"Not at all," she said, still smiling. "Maybe that's part of the point."

He gave her a long look, like he didn't understand. And maybe he didn't. He *was* a demon, after all. Rebellion was in his blood. It wasn't something new for him, let alone something it had taken a few thousand years to come around to.

"I'll look you up sometime," he promised.

"I'd like that," she said. "Until then, think of me on Christmas, all right?"

He looked at her for a long moment with glittering eyes. With a grumble, he swiped one hand across his cheek. It came back wet. "Every time I eat one of those unsatisfying cookies," he said, "or that disgusting mint stick, I'll think of you."

Then he turned away and disappeared around a corner.

She knew she had to get out of here, the sooner the better. But she stayed where she was, looking up at the Christmas lights, trying to figure out what to do next.

She was going to have to disappear. That was a given.

But she stood under the tree for a long moment, breathing in its crisp pine scent, basking in the twinkling glow of the rainbow lights.

Then she soared into the sky again. This time, she stayed lower, and made a pass by some apartment windows. She might as well give people something exciting to talk about. The next morning, they could tell their family they'd seen an angel on Christmas.

Then she sailed higher into the sky. She looked down at the city, at its rainbow glow, at the dusting of snow along its streets. And, far in the distance, the small figure of a demon, catching a snowflake on his forked tongue on his first white Christmas.

THE NAUGHTY LIST

Twinkletoes raced into the barn with panic written over his face. His round glasses were askew, and one of his buttons was buttoned in the wrong hole—which, for Twinkletoes, was tantamount to not being dressed at all. He didn't bother wiping his boots on the mat, and he trailed snowy footprints behind him. No one ever bothered wiping their feet coming into the barn, mind you—it was a barn, after all. No one but Twinkletoes. At the sight of that button and those snowy footprints, Snowdrop looked up in alarm, still clutching the red-wrapped present he had been about to load into the sleigh.

"Emergency! Emergency!" Twinkletoes said, out of breath. He paused to rest his hands on his thighs and draw in a few deep gasps. "Oh, this is very bad."

"Well, are you going to tell us what it is?" Snowdrop

asked. "Or are you just going to stand there panting? We're on a schedule, you know, and we still don't have all the gifts loaded yet."

"I know we're on a schedule!" said Twinkletoes, his eyes bugging out in alarm. "That's why this is so bad! Santa is... he's..."

Snowdrop took him by the shoulders, even though the last thing he wanted to do was touch the other elf. He didn't know whether snootiness was catching, and he didn't care to find out. "Breathe," he ordered Twinkletoes. "Tell me what's wrong. Slowly."

"Santa is *asleep!*" Twinkletoes gasped out. "He won't wake up! And we have to leave within the hour if we have any chance of getting all the gifts out on time!"

The barn filled with gasps. All around Snowdrop, presents hit the barn floor with soft thuds as everyone forgot about filling the sleigh.

"He's asleep?" Gingerbread muttered. "No, no, no. This isn't good."

"What are we going to do?" squeaked Sugarplum. "He's supposed to *drive* this thing!"

Snowdrop didn't panic. He faced Twinkletoes with his trademark calm. This was the attitude that made Santa trust him with the most important jobs—like making sure the sleigh got loaded on time, and handling the rush jobs for toys in unexpectedly high demand. "Show me," he ordered.

Quivering with panic, Twinkletoes led him out of the barn and down the gumdrop path to Santa's gingerbread mansion. Sure enough, there he was, passed out on his cotton-candy couch. He had one arm across his eyes, and his belly quivered with every foundation-shaking snore.

"He must have had too much peppermint ale last night," Twinkletoes fluttered. "I *told* him he shouldn't be drinking."

Snowdrop gingerly reached out and grasped the portly man by the shoulder. He took a deep breath. The smell of stale peppermint slapped him in the face. Santa had overindulged, all right.

Snowdrop shook him, already knowing it wouldn't do any good. Santa only snored louder.

He stepped back and shook his head. "He's not waking up any time soon," he reported to Twinkletoes. "We're going to have to make other arrangements."

He did his best to hide the relief on his face.

He hadn't been sure how effective the sedative would be on someone Santa's size. It had been hard enough to slip it into his peppermint ale in the first place, let alone make sure he used enough to have an effect but not enough that Santa would taste it. It was a good thing peppermint ale tasted so strongly of... well... peppermint.

Twinkletoes paced back and forth, wringing his hands. "Oh no, oh no," he muttered. "What are we going to do?"

Snowdrop paused, tapping his chin, like he was thinking hard. After a moment, he heaved a mighty sigh, like he was preparing to make a difficult but noble sacrifice. "I'll do it," he said in a brave and long-suffering voice.

"You'll do what?" asked Twinkletoes. "Wake him? I thought you said you couldn't!"

"I'll drive the sleigh, of course."

Twinkletoes's eyes got even bigger. "But... but... you're an *elf!* We can't do that! We don't know how!"

"The reindeer know the way," Snowdrop pointed out. "The rest just comes down to putting the right presents under the right tree." He patted his bulging pocket. "I've got the list right here. Checked it twice, too." He shot a glance at Santa's quivering belly. "Besides, we might go faster with me in his place. It'll take a lot less effort for me to fit down the chimneys."

Twinkletoes stared at the unconscious Santa Claus, then at Snowdrop. "Are you sure you can do it?"

Snowdrop gave another loud sigh. "It won't be easy," he said, "but I'll do it. For the children, and for Santa, and for the North Pole."

"You're so brave," Twinkletoes squeaked. Then he straightened up his shoulders and heaved a long-suffering sigh of his own. "I'm... I'm..." he said faintly. "I'm coming with you!"

Snowdrop barely kept himself from screaming. No, that wouldn't do at *all*. "You can't," he said, trying not to sound too desperate. "You need to stay here and keep order. Not to mention tell Santa what's going on when he wakes up."

"No, I have to be there," Twinkletoes insisted. "I'm Santa's second-in-command. It would be a dereliction of duty for me to let someone else do this in my place. Either we do it together, or I go it alone." Just saying those last words made all the color drain from Twinkletoes's face.

And from Snowdrop's. "All right," he said hastily. "You can come. But I don't want any panicking from you while we're up in the sleigh at thirty thousand feet, got it?"

Twinkletoes paled still further, until he was the color of the snow outside. "Does it really go that high?"

"Higher," Snowdrop lied. "Are you sure you want to do this?"

Twinkletoes looked like he was about to throw up. But he nodded. "It's my duty," he said in a tiny voice.

"Then follow me," said Snowdrop, trying to hide his frustration. He strode ahead of Twinkletoes and jogged back to the barn. "Let's go," he called over his shoulder. "We've got a schedule to keep."

When they got back to the barn, the other elves had, of course, completely forgotten about what they were supposed to be doing in their panic. Snowdrop stifled a sigh. This was why Santa relied on him for the high-pressure jobs—because everyone else inevitably got distracted when the stakes got high. He barked orders at the elves—"Gingerbread, start loading that pile of gifts to your right. Sugarplum, handle the stocking stuffers—nice and gentle, now. Twinkletoes here will tell you the new plan."

Twinkletoes opened his mouth, but all that came out was an anemic squeak.

"All right," Snowdrop said, *"I'll* tell you the plan." And he did, to a chorus of shocked and admiring gasps.

He made a quiet-down motion with his hands. "Later," he said brusquely. "If we don't get the sleigh loaded, the plan won't matter. So get to work." Then he dove in and loaded presents alongside the rest of them, double-time.

Twinkletoes, of course, didn't do anything but stand there watching and hyperventilating.

The presents got loaded just in time. The flight team hooked up the reindeer and checked each of them over from nose to hooves, to make sure none of them had developed any last-minute problems. As a final touch,

Candycane tapped Rudolph's nose, just to make sure it was still in top condition. They all breathed a sigh of relief when it lit up a vibrant red.

The flight team checked the sleigh next. "You're ready to go," they informed Snowdrop in a slightly shaky chorus. They knew about the Santa situation by now, too.

Snowdrop climbed into the sleigh. His feet didn't even hit the floor, and he had to lean forward to grasp the reins. This seat was built for someone much bigger than him. But he didn't let his nerves show on his face.

He patted the seat next to him. "Well?" he asked Twinkletoes. "Are you coming?" He hoped the answer would be no.

But Twinkletoes climbed up next to him. "For the North Pole," he said faintly, his face turning a fascinating shade of green.

The reindeer trotted out the barn doors and took off running. "Wait," Twinkletoes squeaked. "I'm not so sure about—"

Too late. The reindeer took off into the sky. A second later, the sleigh followed with a bone-shaking lurch.

Twinkletoes gasped and wheezed. His eyes went even bigger underneath his round glasses. He clamped one hand around his belly, and another over his mouth.

Snowdrop ignored him. As soon as they were up above the clouds, he pulled out his list. Not Santa's list, the one the old man had been lovingly working on all year. This was the other list—his *personal* list. He knew he had the right one—he had checked it twice, after all.

He read off the first address to the reindeer. "And step on it," he added. "We've got quite a few more houses than usual this year."

Twinkletoes gave Snowdrop a nauseated frown. He lifted his hand away from his mouth to say suspiciously, "I don't remember that address being on the list."

"You've got a lot to keep track of," said Snowdrop. "Being Santa's second-in-command, and all."

"No, no, I'm sure," Twinkletoes insisted. "I have an eidetic memory, you know. And that house was *definitely* on the naughty list." He snatched a hand out toward the long scroll of paper clutched in Snowdrop's fingers. "Give me that."

Snowdrop lurched back, making the sleigh wobble precariously. Twinkletoes clapped one hand over his mouth again as he strained for the list with the other. The scroll of paper fluttered in the wind and threatened to sail out of Snowdrop's grip. Snowdrop clutched it harder, crumpling the paper, as he stood on his tiptoes to hold it out of Twinkletoes's reach.

He tried very hard not to look down.

Twinkletoes leapt at him. The sleigh wobbled back and forth like a boat on a stormy sea. With a squeak, Twinkletoes sat down hard in his seat, clapping both hands over his mouth this time.

Snowdrop tucked the list away in his pocket. He sat back down, and breathed a sigh of relief when the sleigh righted itself in short order. "I think it's clear *that* isn't a good idea," he said. "So for the sake of both our lives, sit down and keep quiet for the rest of the ride. You don't need to concern yourself with my list. It looks like you've got your hands full holding in your dinner."

Twinkletoes dropped his hands to his lap and pressed his slender fingers primly together. "Where did you get that list?" he demanded.

"I thought we just agreed we were done fighting over

the list."

Twinkletoes glanced over his shoulder at the back of the sleigh, piled high with presents. "Now that I think about it," he said, "there are an awful lot of presents this year. I *thought* it was taking too long to load the sleigh."

"We had a few new guys on sleigh duty this year. They don't have the hang of it just yet. Couldn't be helped."

Twinkletoes put his hands on his hips. "I didn't get to be Santa's second-in-command by being an idiot, you know. *What* is going on here?"

Well, it looked like the jig was up. Snowdrop sighed. "You weren't supposed to know," he said. "If you hadn't insisted on coming along, you would be waiting down there, none the wiser. You and the big guy both."

Twinkletoes spluttered. It took him a moment to form coherent words. "This... this... this is *insurrection!*" He grabbed for the reins.

"I wouldn't do that." Snowdrop gave the reins a sharp tug. The reindeer obeyed his command, taking off through the sky at double speed. With a gulp, Twinkletoes clutched his stomach.

"Do that again," said Snowdrop, "and I'll make them do a loop-the-loop."

"You wouldn't."

Snowdrop narrowed his eyes at Twinkletoes. "Watch me."

"I'll tell Santa Claus all about this when we get down to the ground," he said in a voice that was no less officious for being squeaky and faintly nauseated. "Don't think I won't. We'll see if he ever puts you in charge of anything again."

"Maybe so," said Snowdrop. "But my work will be

done."

"What is this?" Twinkletoes demanded. "Are you trying to take his job?" His eyes went big again. "Or *mine?* Because I won't hand over my position that easily. Being Santa's second-in-command is a sacred duty. Do all the loop-the-loops you want—I won't surrender."

Snowdrop rolled his eyes. "I don't want your job. And I definitely don't want Santa's. All I want is a little Christmas joy—for *everyone.* This year, we're giving toys to *all* the children—even the naughty ones." His cheeks flushed with pride; he couldn't help it. "I had the elves make extra toys this year, and I got them loaded onto the sleigh. It's a good thing Santa trusts me to handle these things myself."

"You mean... you intend to..." Another round of spluttering followed. "You want to give presents to *naughty children?*" Snowdrop doubted Twinkletoes would have looked quite so poleaxed if Snowdrop had suggested dumping the entire load of presents into the ocean.

"I'm glad we understand each other," said Snowdrop. "Now sit down, be quiet, and don't rock the boat. You're the one who invited yourself along on this little trip."

"But... but... those kids don't deserve presents! It's bad enough that we stopped giving them lumps of coal!"

"Think about it," said Snowdrop. "Do you really want any child to be sad on Christmas, naughty or not? Christmas is about joy and love, isn't it?"

"Well... yes... but we have a reputation to uphold! Kids won't be good if they think they'll get toys no matter what!"

"How many kids do you really think are going to

99

stop being naughty just because they don't want to risk not getting a present?" Snowdrop asked. "Trust me, kids are going to be naughty regardless. Being naughty all year is a lot more satisfying than getting a toy one day out of three hundred and sixty-five. As a former naughty kid myself, I would know."

Twinkletoes shook his head. "You're pulling my leg. I don't believe you were ever naughty. You're the most trusted elf in Santa's Village—or you were before this... this..." His hands fluttered. "This act of *treason*."

"Oh, I was the naughtiest elf child in my village," Snowdrop assured him. He smiled, remembering. "I've always been good at getting things done, it's true—but that just means that when I was naughty, I was better at it than anyone else."

The sleigh sailed downward with a swoop that made Twinkletoes clutched his belly. The sleigh landed on top of a snow-covered roof. Snowdrop stood and hopped out. "Well, here we are," he said. "First stop."

Twinkletoes hopped out the other side. "Not a chance. I won't allow it. You are *not* going down that chimney." He blocked the chimney with his body, adopting a wide-legged stance and spreading his arms in a T.

Snowdrop frowned thoughtfully at Twinkletoes. It looked like the threat of loop-the-loops hadn't been enough. If he wanted his plan to work, he was going to have to find a way to deal with this problem.

When the sleigh took off a few minutes later, there was an extra present under the tree below: a scowling elf bound tightly with multicolored Christmas lights. Maybe Twinkletoes could learn to have some Christmas fun. He could stand to learn a thing or two from a naughty kid.

Snowdrop would pick him up eventually, of course. After all, Christmas was about joy and love—and what would bring Twinkletoes more joy than getting back to his clipboards and schedules? Even if maybe what he deserved was to stay in that house with that naughty child a little while longer.

For now, Snowdrop had to hurry. He had a long list to go through—almost three times as long as usual. It was a good thing he had a reputation for getting things done.

About the Author

Zoe Cannon may or may not be a supervillain out to conquer the world through writing. When not writing, they can be found perfecting their schemes for world domination, plotting against their archenemies, and staying up too late reading a book. Their secret lair is rumored to be located somewhere in southern New Hampshire. They also write as their mild-mannered alter ego, Z.J. Cannon.

Subscribe at https://www.zoecannon.com/newsletter to find out the second a new book comes out, get sneak peeks and opportunities to read upcoming releases early, and find out what projects are in the works. Plus, dog pictures! When you sign up, you'll get a free electronic copy of *No Regrets*, an exclusive introduction to the Iron Bound urban fantasy series.

Also by Zoe Cannon

Story Collections
Lonely Streets
Dark Wings, Bright Flame
Digital Soul
Love Is Strange
Not Your Heroine
The Fire Inside
Digital Flesh
Mortal Creatures
With Friends Like These

Uncollected Short Stories
Safer at Home: A Ghost Story
Second Wave
Inheritance
Safety First

Written as Z.J. Cannon

Nic Ward
Nothing Sacred
Broken Faith
Crooked Idols
Lost Cause
Blood Sacrament
Fallen Saints
Blighted Angels
Sinners' Kingdom

Hound of Hades
Death Trace
Memory Game
Ghost Town
Night Terrors
Hell Bent
Blind Side
Trinity Gambit
Friendly Fire
Bitter Fruit
Skeleton Key
Hound of Hades: The Short Stories

Iron Bound
No Promises
No Illusions
No Sanctuary
No Escape
No Heroes

Milton Keynes UK
Ingram Content Group UK Ltd.
UKHW010935221123
433051UK00001B/60